ONE, TWO, THREE

Fargo sighted the three Blackfoot, aimed his Colt slightly low, allowing for the kick of the gun, and the first Indian's chest erupted in a shower of bone and blood. The other two braves whirled and started toward the sound of the shot, only to be diverted by a horse that Skye let run loose. Skye yanked the thin, double-edged throwing knife from the sheath around his calf as the brave nearest him swerved his horse to chase the one escaping. The knife hurtled into the Blackfoot's back, right between the shoulder blades. Now there was just one left, heading toward Skye with a heavy stone tomahawk in his hand. The Trailsman had to deal with him so that the rest of the Indians couldn't spot his hiding place.

He had to use his raw nerve and bare hands . . .

THE TRAILSMAN RIDES AGAIN

THE TRAILSMAN 80

BLOOD
PASS

by

Jon Sharpe

○
A SIGNET BOOK

NEW AMERICAN LIBRARY

PUBLISHED BY
THE NEW AMERICAN LIBRARY
OF CANADA LIMITED

PUBLISHER'S NOTE

This book is a work of fiction. Names, characters, places, and incidents either are the product of the author's imagination or are used fictitiously, and any resemblance to actual persons, living or dead, events, or locales is entirely coincidental.

NAL BOOKS ARE AVAILABLE AT QUANTITY DISCOUNTS
WHEN USED TO PROMOTE PRODUCTS OR SERVICES.
FOR INFORMATION PLEASE WRITE TO PREMIUM MARKETING DIVISION,
NEW AMERICAN LIBRARY, 1633 BROADWAY,
NEW YORK, NEW YORK 10019.

The first chapter of this book previously appeared in *Smoky Hell Trail*, the seventy-ninth book in this series.

First Printing, August, 1988

2 3 4 5 6 7 8 9

 SIGNET TRADEMARK REG. U.S. PAT OFF. AND FOREIGN COUNTRIES
REGISTERED TRADEMARK — MARCA REGISTRADA
HECHO EN WINNIPEG, CANADA

SIGNET, SIGNET CLASSIC, MENTOR, ONYX, PLUME, MERIDIAN
AND NAL BOOKS are published in Canada by The New American
Library of Canada, Limited, 81 Mack Avenue, Scarborough,
Ontario, Canada M1L 1M8
PRINTED IN CANADA
COVER PRINTED IN U.S.A.

The Trailsman

Beginnings . . . they bend the tree and they mark the man. Skye Fargo was born when he was eighteen. Terror was his midwife, vengeance his first cry. Killing spawned Skye Fargo, ruthless, cold-blooded murder. Out of the acrid smoke of gunpowder still hanging in the air, he rose, cried out a promise never forgotten.

The Trailsman, they began to call him, all across the West: searcher, scout, hunter, the man who could see where others only looked, his skills for hire but not his soul, the man who lived each day to the fullest, yet trailed each tomorrow. Skye Fargo, the Trailsman, the seeker who could take the wildness of a land and the wanting of a woman and make them his own.

*1860 the edge of the Bitterroot Mountains,
a land still part of the Oregon Territory
but called Idaho by Indians, missionaries,
fur trappers and all who braved
its untamed fierceness . . .*

1

The big man's eyes snapped open at the sound.

But he lay very still in the woodland glen, senses alert. Unmoving, he let his wild-creature hearing define the sound, let it take shape and form. It wasn't a raccoon, marten, or possum—no small creature. The steps were too heavy for a deer. An elk or a moose, he reasoned, and instantly corrected the thought. The steps were not cautious enough. He continued to listen and pursed his lips. A horse, with a rider. A horse moved differently without someone on its back.

Slowly he pushed himself up on one elbow, the big Colt in his hand. He peered through the brush. The early-morning mists still hugged the ground, wispy trails, not unlike a giant, frayed scarf. It was unusually warm for October—Indian summer, most folks called it. He called it one of Mother Nature's tricks. The horse appeared, legs enshrouded by the mist, looking as though it were floating along the ground. He saw the rider and stiffened. A frown swept across his brow. He rubbed one big hand across his eyes and peered through the early morning again, wondering whether the mists had played tricks on him.

But they hadn't, and Skye Fargo felt astonishment sweep through him again. The rider was a girl. That didn't amaze him. He'd seen girl riders in the early morning before. But this one was stark-naked, absolutely and totally nude. He stared at her slender and shapely body—small perfect breasts, beautiful legs, a flat stomach, and long, slightly scraggly blond hair around a face that seemed hardly more than fifteen.

She rode bareback, appropriately enough. He grunted and stayed transfixed as she disappeared into the forest, still moving with slow, airy deliberateness.

"Damn," Fargo swore softly, and pushed to his feet. He pulled on clothes, tossed his bedroll over the magnificent Ovaro with the jet black fore- and hindquarters and gleaming white midsection. He swung onto the horse and moved through the forest after the girl. The dewy morning grass clearly showed the marks of her horse's steps and Fargo followed the trail through the woods until he hurriedly reined up at the edge of a small cleared space around a tiny forest pond. The girl rested on a stone at the edge of the pond, an unruly lock of blond hair hanging over her face. She put her head back, her eyes half-closed, thin arms stretched out for support. Her small breasts were perfectly shaped little white mounds, each piquantly peaked with a very light-pink tip.

She was like an elfin creature who had suddenly emerged from a forest bower, a wood sprite that might vanish if he tried to approach closer. His eyes flicked to the horse and he saw an old mare with knobs on her knees and a coat that badly needed brushing. Nothing elfin about the horse, he grunted, and brought his eyes back to the girl. She leaned to one side, both breasts dipping beautifully, pulled up a blade of grass, and sucked on it with Cupid's-bow lips that made her face suddenly sensuous in a strange girl-woman way. Fargo slid silently from the Ovaro and stepped into the cleared space. The naked wood sprite looked up, light-blue eyes neither frightened nor particularly startled. "Hello," he said.

"Hello," she answered, her voice thin. She remained unmoving and met his stare as though she were fully clothed, and he felt himself frowning.

"That's quite a riding outfit," he remarked.

"My favorite," she said with a smile that managed to be both shy and suggestive.

"You always ride around like that?" he asked.

"At this hour, here in the woods," she said. "It's

wonderful. You feel free and natural, like being one with everything in the forest."

He studied her, and her light-blue eyes returned his appraisal. She had a way of seeming as simple as a child and as wise as a woman, a combination he realized was very exciting. "You have a name?" he asked.

"Cassie," she murmured, and her eyes continued to appraise him. "What's your name?" she asked with direct simpleness.

"Fargo, Skye Fargo," he said. "You ever think you could get into trouble riding around like that?"

"You're the first person I've ever met at this hour of the morning," she said. "I've often wondered what I'd do if I did meet someone." She smiled and the smile held a sensuous pixiness in it.

"Doesn't seem to bother you any talking to me like that," Fargo commented.

"Does it bother you?" she asked slyly.

"Maybe," he allowed.

Her smile widened. "Good, because I suddenly want to make love, right here and now," Cassie said.

Fargo's gaze narrowed at her. "You often get these sudden urges?" he asked.

She shrugged, sat up straighter, and her breasts seemed to dance. "You think I shouldn't talk this way," she said with a sudden half-pout, suddenly child-like again.

"Didn't say that," Fargo returned.

She stood up, held her girl-woman body very straight, slender legs slightly spread, flat little belly thrust forward, a small but very black triangle a sharp contrast to her milk-white skin. Again she seemed almost unreal, a woodland mirage. "It'd be natural, completely natural and simple, the way it ought to be," she said. "Don't you feel it, Fargo? Doesn't it reach you?"

"Something sure as hell is reaching me, honey," Fargo said, and he stepped toward her, his loins throbbing.

She took a step backward and lowered herself to the grass, her smile radiating girl-woman bewitchment.

She lay back, stretched the nymphlike body, arms raised over her head as he pulled off clothes. Never turn away from something just because you don't expect it, he reminded himself as he dropped to his knees beside her. She brought her thin arms down, encircling his neck as he lay half over her and felt the smooth, soft babylike warmth of her skin. He bent his face down, took one small, peaked breast in his mouth, circled his lips around the light-pink tip, and felt her slender legs move under him.

"Don't wait. Now, now," she murmured to his surprise. He shifted himself over her. Both of her hands clasped his head, palms flattened against his temples, sliding down to his face, all but covering his ears. He felt her slender, flat-bellied body thrust up against him as she continued to clasp his face. He never heard the blow that crashed against the back of his head, but he felt her hands still half over his ears and then the sharp, shooting pain as the world went dark.

Dimly he felt himself being pushed to the ground, and he tried to struggle to his knees in the black void. Another sharp burst of pain shot through him, then he felt only blankness, the utter void of time, place, and feeling.

He didn't know how long he'd lain there, but the pain returned with a slow, tickling sensation. He wondered how pain could tickle. Yet it did, in its own way, moving through his fingers, up his arms, spotting his legs. He forced his eyes open and let the world slowly take shape, become trees, leaves, branches. He started to sit up and cried out at the bolt that shot through the back of his head. He lay back again, his eyes open, cheek against the coolness of the grass. The pain slowly became bearable and he sat up once more.

He looked around and recognized the tiny pond and the stone. But the girl, the elfin wood sprite, was gone. So was nearly everything else. His gun, gun belt, clothes, and boots had vanished. He peered at the Ovaro. His saddle was gone, along with all his gear and the big Sharps in its saddle case. He rose, winced, and straightened up as rage pushed pain aside. He had been drawn into a trap, led into it with a ploy no man could resist. "Wood sprite," he muttered aloud. "Bushwhacking little bitch." He walked to the Ovaro and pulled himself onto the horse, instantly feeling the warmth of the fur and hide against his buttocks and legs.

He glanced up at the sun. He'd been out for the better part of the morning, so he spurred the Ovaro forward, his eyes like ice as they scanned the ground. Suddenly he appreciated the warmth of Indian summer as he found the tracks of the girl's horse and followed the trail. He reined to a halt where she had stopped, and he saw additional hoofprints. By skirting the spot, he saw where they had ridden off together. There had been at least three horses, perhaps four; their prints were too close together to be sure.

They had stayed in the forest for a while, but eventually the prints emerged onto flat plains and led straight toward Ridersville. Fargo reined up. He had planned to make Ridersville himself before dusk, but that was when he had clothes. He turned the pinto around and went back into the trees. He dismounted inside the treeline and grimaced at his nakedness as he stared into the horizon. Maybe he could sneak into town in the dead of night and find something to wear. He pondered this but immediately discarded the thought. Ridersville was the kind of gateway town that never slept. There'd be no chance to sneak in stark-naked, not at any hour. Besides, he reminded himself, he hadn't a cent with which to buy a pair of Levi's. Damn that little wood-nymph bitch, he swore silently.

But if she and her friends had ridden into Ridersville, there was a good chance it was to sell his saddle—and everything else. He had to follow the trail, but first he had to find some clothes. He lowered himself onto a smooth rock and settled down, waiting and gazing across the plains that spread in front of him. A woman driving a buckboard went by in the distance. A half-hour later, four cowhands turned and headed toward town. Just as he'd decided to ride the pinto farther along the perimeter of the trees, a Conestoga moved slowly from left to right in the distance, silhouetted by the setting sun. He watched the lone wagon roll across the plains toward the foothills of the Beaverhead range in the far distance. As the sun lowered, the wagon grew dim and finally disappeared in the shroud of night.

If they were headed toward the Beaverhead range, he knew they'd have to camp for the night. When the moon rose he climbed onto the pinto and rode from the trees. Indian summer was a daytime event, he took note as he felt the chill of night on his naked body. He scanned the ground, easily picking up the wagon-wheel marks until he spotted the Conestoga pulled off at the edge of the trees. A lamp was still hanging from the front of the wagon, so he veered the Ovaro into the trees until he was closer to the wagon. He dismounted, crouched, and waited. Finally an arm reached out from the front of the wagon and took the lamp inside. Minutes later, the light went out and Fargo settled down to wait again. Everyone had to be asleep when he went to the wagon. When the moon was almost overhead, he crept to the rear corner of the old Conestoga.

He moved on catlike steps and pulled up one corner of canvas to peer into the back. He frowned as he saw two steamer trunks and a stack of hatboxes atop them. His eyes went to the top edge of the canvas but he saw no clothes hanging to dry overnight. The trunk would be impossible to move in silence, so he reached for the top hatbox. It was large enough to hold more than a hat, and he carefully slid it toward him. He had it half out of the opening in the canvas when a voice snapped from the darkness.

"Drop that box or I shoot."

Fargo flung himself sideways and rolled on the grass as he let the box topple to the ground. He came up behind the team of horses and crouched there as the figure swung to the ground from the tail of the Conestoga. A thin ray of moonlight showed brown, shoulder-length hair and a long robe that reached to the ankles. The woman moved closer and he saw the big Hawkins in her hands. She was young, with good, even features in her face, attractive even in the pale light of the half-moon. "Come out here where I can see you," she ordered.

"I don't think you want that," Fargo said. "I don't have a stitch on."

"Good try," she sniffed. "Now you get out here or I come after you shooting."

Fargo shrugged and moved away from the horses. He caught her quick hissed gasp of surprise as she stared at him. "Told you so, honey," he said.

"Get behind the horses again," she ordered, but he saw her glance linger at every part of his muscled body. He moved behind the rump of the nearest horse and saw that she kept the rifle level at him.

"I was trying to get some clothes," Fargo said.

"What happened to yours?" she asked.

Fargo grimaced. "You're not going to believe this," he said.

"Try me," she answered, so he took a deep breath and began to recount his misadventure, starting from the moment he'd first seen the blond wood sprite riding naked through the morning mists. He drew another deep breath when he finished.

"Told you you wouldn't believe me. Can't say I blame you," he said.

Her eyes peered at him for another moment. "I believe you," she said.

"You do?" he blurted. "Why?" he asked out of astonished curiosity.

"That story's too damn wild to make up and too ridiculous to use," she said. "It has to be true."

Fargo managed a smile. "You're very sharp," he said. "And I'm glad for that. The whole thing's made me feel like a damn fool."

"Serves you right," she sniffed, and he frowned

15

back. "But then you're all the same, always panting to please yourselves."

"I don't believe in passing up opportunities," he said.

"Even a mouse knows to sniff around before he grabs a piece of cheese," she tossed back disdainfully.

Skye swore silently at the truth of her sharpness. "I still need some clothes," he grumbled, and she finally lowered the big Hawkins.

"Just so happens I'm on my way to meet up with some other wagons. I'm bringing supplies, lots of different things," she said, casting another appraising glance at his chest and shoulders. "You're big, but I've got some things that might fit well enough," she said, and quickly climbed back into the Conestoga. She turned on a lamp and he saw her shadow rummaging through boxes. Finally she leaned out and tossed him a pair of trousers, a jacket, and two dirty boots. He sat down and pulled them on. The boots fit best, for the trousers barely closed and the jacket was drawn tight across his chest. She gazed at him when he stepped from behind the horses.

"They'll do," he said. "Much obliged."

"Some of my brother's things."

Fargo threw a glance at the wagon. "But you're alone," he said.

"Until I join the other wagons," she answered.

"If you tell me where, I'll try to get these back to you," he said.

"No need, really. They're extras," she said. "But we're meeting at Beaverhead, alongside the Madison."

"What do you know? The world's full of coincidences," Fargo said. "I was heading that way myself. Maybe I will be able to get these things back to you."

She shrugged. "We won't be staying there long," she said.

"What's your name, 'case I get there in time," he said.

"Hope Maxwell," she said. "You're welcome to bed

down here. I've an extra blanket and the night wind's getting sharp."

He thought for a moment. Chances were he'd find out little in Ridersville in the middle of the night and would have to wait for morning, anyway. "I'd be obliged again," he said, and this time she stepped from the wagon and brought him the blanket. She had round brown eyes, slightly rounded cheeks, and a short nose with a little tilt to the end of it. It was a very attractive face. "Tell me one thing." He smiled. "I'm usually too quiet for most folks to hear. How'd you pick up I was moving that hatbox?"

"I was awake the whole time. I knew I was being followed from the moment I settled down for the night," she said. His eyes questioned her. "Call it a sixth sense," she said. "I've always had it, a kind of inner knowing. More than intuition. It scares me sometimes."

He nodded, and her brown eyes held his for a moment longer.

"Good night," she said and climbed into the wagon.

He smiled as he lay down with the blanket just beside the wheels. She hadn't asked his name. It was a strange passing incident and she'd make no more of it. There was a determination under her acuteness. She was on her way to a rendezvous and she'd not let herself be drawn into any detours, no matter how intriguing they might be. But she'd been generous and he was grateful to her. He closed his eyes and sleep came to him at once.

Only the sharp bark of prairie dogs interrupted his slumber. The wagon was still and he rose, folded the blanket, and pulled aside a part of the canvas flap at the tail gate. She lay asleep on a mattress on the wagon floor, her brown hair falling loosely around her face. Her cheeks were rounder in the light of dawn than they'd seemed in the moonlight shadows; she was prettier. But even asleep, the determination was in her face, and he silently backed from the wagon, climbed onto the Ovaro, and sent the horse at a slow walk across the plains.

He rode with his lake-blue eyes hardening, the line of his jaw growing tight. Chasing down a blonde, bushwhacking wood nymph was a first for him, he grunted. But he'd sure as hell chase her down.

2

The ill-fitting clothes pulled uncomfortably around him as he rode. His thoughts wandered to the towering mountains that stretched as far as he could see in the distance. To the north, the Bitterroot range rose upward while to the south the Salmon River Mountains all but blanketed the distant sky. They were all part of the great Rocky Mountains that cut the land in two like a giant fence. They offered only death and disaster to those who dared to cross their rugged fierceness, and agonizing, exhausting months of danger, fatigue and failure to those who elected to go around them.

Fargo's lake-blue eyes narrowed as he scanned the land, but rode unhurriedly and enjoyed the sight of the morning mists evaporating in the sun.

The Indians had named this land Idaho, meaning "the place where the sun comes down the mountains." It was a name well given, he reflected as he watched the morning sun roll down the distant peaks. The Nez Percé, the Northern Shoshoni, and the Blackfoot called the mountains theirs, with the Crow and Assiniboin occasionally roaming through. The Northern Shoshoni held the Salmon River Mountains, the Nez Percé ruled the Bitterroot range, and the Blackfoot stayed farther east along the Flathead and into Montana. But they overlapped and each held their own sacred places and special hunting lands throughout the vast mountain ranges and lush valleys.

Fargo started to open one of the buttons on the jacket and grunted as it popped off. He rode across the brown grass, and when the town appeared to his right, he shifted direction and hurried forward, slowing when he entered the single, wide main street. Ridersville was a gateway town, a place where wagons stopped to restock supplies, gather things forgotten, and make repairs before setting off into the wild Northwest. It was a town full of constant activity, bursting with those eager to go on and those relieved to get back. He saw prospectors, trappers, mountain men, and families of pioneers in a sea of Conestogas.

But it wasn't his kind of town, Fargo murmured. Gateway towns such as Ridersville always attracted too many drifters, men waiting to take advantage of those filled with honest innocence and eager hope. As he walked the Ovaro through the crowded main street, he scanned the faces of everyone on foot and hanging from wagons. None of them even faintly resembled the small, straggly-haired blonde. Finally he reined to a halt where a white-aproned man leaned against a barber pole. " 'Morning," he said. "If I had some gear to sell, a saddle and maybe a six-gun or some clothes, where'd I go to in town?"

"Abe Hammond's Trading Post," the man said. "End of town."

"Thank you kindly," Fargo called back, and moved on, skirting a long four-wheel log truck heavily loaded and drawn by six oxen. He rode forward through the rest of town until he reached the last building, a long, flat-roofed structure with the words TRADING POST carved on a slab of wood over the doorway. He dismounted and went in to find one long room filled with low, wood tables covered with an astonishing array of goods. A quick glance showed him every variety of clothing: jackets, fur parkas, shirts, Levi's, hats, and boots. Other counters held trapping gear, snowshoes, shovels, and a hundred more items. Against the walls of the store he saw saddles hung on wall pegs, along with bridles, bits, and stirrups, and dozens of pelts.

He approached a long counter at the rear of the room where a man with frazzled hair and a sharp face watched him through beady eyes that peered over sagging cups of flesh, giving him a dyspeptic expression. On the wall behind the man, Fargo saw an array of revolvers, and he spotted his big Colt at once, hung from a peg on the lowest rung.

"Do something for you, mister?" the man inquired.

"You can," Fargo said, and his eyes traveled to the saddles against the side wall. He saw his immediately, the big Sharps still in its saddlecase hanging beside it. "That Colt on the first peg and that saddle there," he said.

"Finest in the store. Just came in yesterday," the man said. "You've got a good eye, mister."

"I should. They're mine," Fargo said, and the man's eyes showed a flicker of surprise. "Get some clothes along with them?" Fargo questioned.

"Matter of fact, I did. Right over there," the man said, and nodded toward a nearby counter.

Fargo's lips tightened as he saw his things. "That Sharps in the case, too," Fargo said. "All mine and all stolen from me."

"That so?" the man said blandly, and Fargo peered at his pinched face with its sour expression.

"It is," he said. "You're Abe Hammond, I take it." The man nodded, a slightly pained expression coming into his face. "You ever ask about the stuff you buy?" Fargo said.

"Nope," Abe Hammond said.

"You mean you don't want to know if it's stolen?" Fargo snapped back.

"You know how many times I've heard that stolen story, mister?" Abe Hammond said. "Man bets everything he has on a card game and then comes along and says he was robbed. Or he gets rolled by some fancy woman and shows up here with the same story."

"I'm telling you the truth," Fargo said.

"That's what they all say," Abe Hammond sneered.

Fargo's eyes narrowed. "Maybe there's an edge of truth in what you're saying but it's a thin edge," he snapped.

"Meaning what?" the man asked.

21

"You don't give a damn whether what you buy is stolen or not," Fargo said.

Abe Hammond's shrug was an admission. "I believe in the honesty of people," he said.

"Shit you do. You believe in making a good buy," Fargo said. "And those are still my things you have there."

Abe Hammond shrugged again. "You want 'em you'll have to buy 'em back," he said.

"All right. Can't say I like having to buy back my own things, but I'll do it. Soon as I get my money back I'll come pay you," Fargo said.

"Cash on the barrelhead, mister," Abe Hammond said.

Fargo leveled a long stare at the man. "Small girl, pretty face with scraggly blond hair, sell those things to you?" he asked.

"I don't remember faces," Abe Hammond said.

Fargo grunted. It was another of Abe Hammond's convenient answers. The man knew only one thing: a quick buy for as little money as possible. Hammond had him in a bind. Fargo hadn't the money to buy his things back and he couldn't go after the bushwhackers without them. He'd give Abe another chance, though he knew it was as useless as trying to squeeze tears from a rock. "The name's Fargo . . . Skye Fargo. I'm a man known for keeping his word. Give me my things and I'll pay you back," he said.

"I'm a man known for taking cash only," Abe Hammond replied.

Fargo drew a deep sigh, glanced at his saddle on the wall again, and knew he had no choice. He turned to Abe Hammond and shrugged. "Guess I'll have to find some cash," he said.

"Do it fast," the man said. "I get a customer for that saddle or the rifle and they're gone."

Fargo nodded, started to turn away, then he whipped his body around with the speed of an uncoiling rattlesnake. His hands closed around Hammond's neck, and he lifted as he pulled. The trader came halfway across

22

the counter, surprise widening his pouched eyes. Fargo's grip tightened.

"Who sold you my things, goddammit?" he hissed through lips that hardly moved.

The man's face began to grow red as his breath became a trickle of air. "No . . . no . . . names . . ." he gasped.

Fargo loosened his hold a fraction. "Was it a little blonde?" he barked.

The man managed to shake his head. "She . . . she waited . . . outside," he squeezed out.

Fargo shook Hammond as a terrier shakes a rat. "Who sold it to you?" he pressed.

"Two fellers . . . fat . . . brought the stuff in," Abe Hammond croaked out.

Fargo relaxed his grip some more and let the man gulp in air. "They sold you other things," he said, and Abe Hammond's eyes grew crafty and Fargo's hands tightened around his throat at once. "When, damn you? Don't get smart with me," Fargo warned, and the man's eyes began to bulge.

"All right," he gasped. "Last few weeks . . . every few days."

"You knew it had to be stolen gear, you miserable money-hungry viper," Fargo growled, and felt his fury spiral. He yanked Abe Hammond forward and the man began to fall facedown over the front edge of the counter. Fargo released his grip and brought up a short, curving uppercut that cracked against Abe Hammond's jaw. When the man hit the floor he was unconscious, his legs still up against the side of the counter.

Fargo stepped back, retrieved his clothes, pulled them on, then took his gun belt and Colt and strapped both in place. He took his saddle and the Sharps from the wall and started from the store. He closed the door behind him, walked to the Ovaro, and quickly saddled the horse. He had just finished when he saw a man walking toward the trading post with two ponchos slung over one arm.

"Come back in fifteen minutes," Fargo called. "Abe

23

Hammond's resting. He's feeling poorly." The man nodded and turned away and Fargo swung onto the Ovaro. He rode easily out of town, stayed on a dirt road that grew narrow and finally turned into trees that climbed a low hill. He found a place to halt between two large red cedars, swung to the ground, and sat down against the reddish bark. Abe Hammond's words had been a confirmation of what he had already been certain. The bushwhacking had been no isolated incident. He had been the last of a series of victims. But that offered him his chance to strike back, he murmured in satisfaction.

Cassie and her two helpers set themselves up in the forest land that most riders passed through on their way to town. They watched and waited and all little Cassie had to do was to wander through the morning mists until she passed within sight of someone. It was not unlike fishing, dragging a coachman fly through a trout stream. You were bound to pick up a bite. From there Cassie followed a prearranged pattern.

Fargo's lips grew thin. This time he'd do some following of his own. He stayed against the cedar until the day began to edge into the late afternoon before he rose, climbed onto the Ovaro, and began the ride back to the forest land where he'd bedded down the night before.

The lavender gray of twilight had descended when he reached the area, and using his special talent to recall a trail once ridden and a place once seen, invoking all the skills that made him the Trailsman, he found his way to the tiny, forest pond. He led the Ovaro back into the thick trees beyond the pond, dismounted, and let the horse satisfy himself in a patch of sweet clover. Fargo settled down for the night in the dense foliage, and when darkness came, he put his bedroll down as the night wind grew sharp, a quick reminder that winter lay in wait. But he slept soundly in the still forest and woke with the early dawn.

After stretching and using his canteen to wash and

freshen up, he lay down in the brush on his stomach and waited as the sun began to slide over the land. The warmth of Indian summer crept up again, and the last of the dawn mists clung as wispy fragments in the brush.

Suddenly Fargo heard the soft but definite sound of a horse moving toward the pond, and he rose to see her riding slowly. He swore silently at the wood nymph, at the naked loveliness of her. She halted by the pond and slid from the horse, her small breasts bouncing with perky insouciance. She knelt down on the stone beside the pond but Fargo's eyes were on the trees as the horse and rider appeared. He saw an ordinary-looking cowhand, young and clean-shaven, with eyes bulging as he stared at Cassie. Fargo moved closer to the cowboy, who had left his horse and advanced toward Cassie. She had swung onto the grass, waiting, a faint smile edging her lips.

"Goddamn." The cowpoke frowned.

"We can talk later," Cassie murmured. "Take me first. I want to be taken."

The cowpoke tossed aside his gun belt, yanked off Levi's and boots in eager haste. "Whatever you say, girlie," the man said.

Cassie lay back, both legs held together but raised. Fargo moved still closer as the cowhand almost ran at her, dropped to his knees, and threw himself atop her. Cassie still held her legs together, Fargo noted, but soon her arms came up, her hands clasped the man's face, moved to cover his ears.

"Slow, lover, be careful, slow," Cassie murmured, and kept her hands pressed against both sides of the man's face.

"Jesus," the cowpoke muttered. "Come on, baby." He lifted his buttocks and tried to spear her, but he was too eager, fumbling in desire and haste.

Fargo's gaze went past the man to the two figures emerging from the brush, both barefoot, both crouching as they ran. Abe Hammond's description had been accurate. They were both fat, heavy-paunched, both with small heads for their bodies. But they moved with surprising speed and silence, and Fargo saw one bring the butt of a five-shot, side-hammer Joslyn army revolver down on the back of the cowpoke's head. The man fell limp at once and Cassie pushed herself out from under him, leapt to her feet, and stepped to one side. The two paunchy figures fell upon the prone figure of the cowpoke like vultures on a corpse, instantly stripping clothes away, tossing the shirt to Cassie, who put it on.

Fargo stepped out of the brush, the Colt in his hand. "That's enough, you thievin' sidewinders," he barked, and the two men froze for an instant, slowly straightened up, and turned to him. "Drop your guns," Fargo ordered, and both men obeyed after a glance at the unwavering barrel of the Colt. Fargo saw the small heads held faces that were remarkably alike, both puffy-cheeked with flat noses and tiny blue eyes with a dull-wittedness to them. One had short black hair, the other had a mane of uncombed untidiness. Both wore baggy black trousers and gray shirts, and he guessed each to tip the scales at about two hundred fifty pounds.

Fargo shot a glance at Cassie and saw her watching with wide eyes. "Remember me, honey?" he asked, but she only stared back at him. He returned his gaze to the two men. "I had two hundred dollars on me. I want it back, along with whatever you got for selling my things in town," Fargo said.

"Don't have it," the one with the short hair said, his voice flat, dull, echoing the blankness of his eyes.

"Spent it," the other one said.

"The money," Fargo growled. "I'm not asking again."

The one with the untidy hair shrugged in protest and his paunch shook. "We spent it," he said. "Ask her."

Fargo glanced at Cassie. In the cowpoke's shirt she looked like a shy ten-year-old playing grown-up in her father's clothes. But she nodded, her face grave.

"Then I'll take whatever you have now, for starters. Empty your pockets," Fargo ordered.

26

"You can't take our money," the one with the unruly hair protested. Fargo raised the Colt a fraction of an inch and fired. The man screamed in pain as he clasped a hand to his ear. "Ow, Jesus," he yelled, and drew his hand back and stared at the blood on his fingers. Slowly, his eyes moved to the big man with the gun, and his face wore the expression of a child who thought himself wrongly chastised. "Aw, what'd you do that for?" he complained.

"The next one's between your eyes," Fargo growled, but the man only stared back with the eyes of a slightly dull, uncomprehending child. Fargo frowned at the one with the short hair as he turned to him, anger flooding his puffy-cheeked face.

"Damn you, you hurt him. You hurt Zeb," he roared, gathering himself to charge, but stopping as he saw the Colt leveled at him. "Damn you," he muttered, but stayed in place.

"Empty your pockets, both of you," Fargo said. "This is the last time I'm going to say it." Both stared back at him and again he saw the strange dullard's expression in their eyes. But it was mixed with a craftiness that showed they had learned to survive.

"Damn," the one muttered again, and started to empty his pockets.

"You gonna let him rob us, Zane?" the one with the creased ear protested.

"Dammit, Zeb, he's gonna shoot clear through us if we don't do what he says," Zane answered.

"Couldn't have said it better myself," Fargo commented, and watched them both empty their pockets.

Cassie stayed unmoving, looking on with her light-blue eyes still round. She somehow managed to seem removed from all that had happened and at the same time very much a part of it.

Zeb and Zane put the contents of their pockets on the ground and Fargo saw a key ring, a pad of tobacco, cigarette papers, rubber bands, and with surprise, a half-dozen marbles. He also saw them empty out two rolls of bills that he guessed came close to a hundred dollars.

"Get back," he ordered, and Zane moved first, Zeb with more reluctance. Fargo took a long step forward, scooped up the money, and pushed it into his pocket. He caught the movement of Zeb's feet as the man dug into the ground and charged, head lowered. Fargo stepped back from the bull-like charge and brought his left up in a short, whistling blow that met Zeb's jaw. The man shuddered to a halt, swayed, staggered backward, and dropped to one knee where he stayed for a moment, shaking his head and sending little spatters of blood from his ear.

The other one hurried over to him and helped him to his feet. "No more, Zeb," he murmured solicitously. "He's got that six-gun, remember. You're only gonna get yourself shot."

"Better listen to the man," Fargo said. He watched Zane pulled Zeb away. Both moved back like two reluctant fat boars. Fargo's glance went to Cassie; her eyes hadn't moved from him. "You want to tell me some more about this little scheme?" he said. "Before I take you all in to the sheriff in Ridersville."

The voice cut in before Cassie could answer, low and rumbling but definitely a woman's voice. "Drop that gun, mister," it said. "You're not takin' anybody anyplace, especially not my boys."

Fargo hesitated but the woman was directly behind him and he slowly let the Colt drop from his fingers. He stepped back, turned, and saw the woman step from the trees. He gawked at a huge shape, at least six-feet-three-inches tall and nearly three hundred pounds, he guessed. A long, one-piece, loose black dress covered her huge body almost to the ground but couldn't hide massive breasts that swayed ponderously as she walked. She held a heavy Hawkens rifle, a gun that could stop a buffalo at close range. She frowned at him out of a wide face with heavy cheekbones, a flat nose, a large mouth, and the same small eyes Zeb and Zane had. There was no slow-wittedness in them, though, just a cold and cruel iciness. Long, matted black hair crowded her face, adding to her wild harridan appearance.

"We made a mistake. We should've killed you," she said, and her small eyes blazed in the wide, heavy face.

"You said there'd be no killin'," Cassie spoke up, and Fargo glanced at her in surprise.

"This one's different. He hurt Zeb," the woman rasped. "Besides, since when do you get to say what I do?" Fargo saw the girl tighten her lips and look away. "And he followed us. He's too smart," the woman added. Her eyes stayed on Fargo, the rifle motionless in her big hands. "Give the boys their money back," she rasped.

"My money," Fargo said.

"Give it back, damn you. I don't want it covered with your blood," the huge woman shouted.

"Understandable. Me neither," Fargo said, and pulled the two rolls of bills out of his pocket and dropped them on the ground a few inches from his left foot.

"You're a real smart-ass bastard, aren't you, mister?" the woman snarled.

"No compliments, please," Fargo said.

"Pick up the money, Zeb," she ordered, and the man started forward, a slight waddle to his gait. Fargo's eyes narrowed and his muscles grew taut. This would be his one chance, he was certain. The huge, wild harridan of a woman had meant her threat. He watched Zeb as the man reached him and bent his fat, paunchy body over to pick up the money. Fargo erupted in a downward spring that used all the strength of his powerful thighs.

His arms closed around Zeb's neck and he pulled the man down on top of him as he hit the ground on his back. Prepared for the man's weight, his abdominal muscles tightened to pine-board hardness. He lay with both hands on the man's jaw and twisted Zeb's head sideways from underneath the paunchy body. "You shoot me, you'll have to shoot through him," Fargo said, and saw the frustrated fury sweep through the huge woman's wide face.

"Ow, Jesus," Zeb swore as Fargo twisted his head and neck an inch farther.

"Now you throw that rifle away or I'm going to twist his fat head right off his shoulders, lady," Fargo said, and Zeb emitted another strangled gasp of pain. "You'll be able to hear his neck break from there," Fargo said. He waited a moment more, barely able to see the woman past Zeb's shoulder. But he watched her face twitch in fury and helplessness, and with a half-roar she flung the rifle aside.

Fargo released his grip on Zeb's head, pushed, and threw the heavy form from him and leapt to his feet as Zane made a flying dive for the rifle. Fargo met the man's dive with his knee and Zane gasped an oath in pain as the blow slammed into his face. He fell sideways, cursed again, and came up on one knee with blood running down one of his puffy cheeks.

Fargo scooped up the rifle, moved on catlike steps, retrieved his Colt in one sweeping motion, and brought both guns up to face the huge woman. Zeb and Zane fell back almost to her side and she dwarfed their paunchy forms.

They stared at him from hurt, frowning faces, Zane using his shirttail to wipe the blood from his cheek. But the huge woman's eyes were icy pinpoints of hate mixed with grudging respect.

"You're a real hard one, aren't you, mister?" she muttered.

"Some folks inspire me," Fargo said. "Who the hell are you?"

"Ma Cowley," she said, and managed a certain pride in her voice.

"You run this thieving operation, it's plain to see," Fargo said, and she nodded. "And these two half-wits?" Fargo asked, and gestured toward Zeb and Zane.

"You watch your mouth, mister," Ma Cowley snapped. "They're my boys."

Fargo glanced at Cassie, who still waited to one side looking like a lost waif. "She's not yours," he said.

"She's my niece," the woman said. "How'd you know she weren't mine?"

"Never saw a Clydesdale foal a race horse," Fargo answered.

"Bastard," the huge woman hissed.

"Much obliged," Fargo said. "Now we'll all go into town together. I just hope the sheriff has a cell big enough for you, Ma." He turned, unloaded the Hawkens, and tossed it back to the huge woman. Zane picked it from the ground. "Mount up," Fargo said, and swung onto the Ovaro and kept the Colt aimed at the others. "You, too, Cassie, honey. You're the star of this show."

"I just do what I'm told," Cassie said, and pulled herself onto her horse.

"Then you'd best pick better company next time around," Fargo said.

"I'm not walkin' all the way to town," Ma Cowley said. "I've got a wagon stopped a few hundred yards away."

"Lead the way. No tricks, none of you. My trigger finger's real itchy," Fargo warned. He swung in behind the others as they walked their horses behind the massive form of Ma Cowley. She led the way to a wagon, a splintered, sagging old Spring wagon with cut-under wheels. Makeshift top bows had been rigged to support a cover but only a few tattered bits of canvas remained attached to the rear bow. The woman climbed aboard it and the wagon frame sagged another two inches.

"Head out," Fargo said, and hung back while the woman moved the wagon forward, down a slope to the road to Ridersville. Zeb and Zane rode beside the wagon, Cassie a few feet away. She rode silently, her eyes lowered, and he almost felt sorry for her. She could reach out with that feeling of waiflike helplessness. But he reminded himself how well she'd played her role in the entire scheme. Feeling sorry for little Cassie was misplacing sympathy, he decided, and rode on with his jaw tight.

The buildings of Ridersville finally came into view and Ma Cowley called back to him without turning around. "You got us all wrong, you know, mister," the huge woman said.

"Sure, this is just a new way of being good samaritans," Fargo called back.

"We just needed to get some money together," the woman said.

"You could've let fat and fatter get themselves a job," Fargo returned.

"Didn't have enough time. We needed money fast," Ma Cowley answered, and turned in the seat of the wagon to look back at him. "You got your things back, and the money. You've no call to turn us in," she said. "You go your way and we'll go ours."

"And you'll keep on bushwhacking people with little Cassie as bait," Fargo said.

"No, today would've been the last one. We just wanted a little extra change," the woman said.

"Well, now you'll get some free room and board," Fargo said as they reached the first buildings of town.

"You don't know as much as you think you do, big man," Ma Cowley sneered, and Fargo ignored the remark as mere bravado.

"Pull up right there," he said as he saw the sheriff's office sign on a narrow building.

Ma Cowley braked the wagon to a halt while Zeb, Zane, and Cassie gathered around her. A man wearing a deputy's badge emerged from the building; he was on the young side with a weak mouth and slack jaw. He took in the huge woman and the others and brought his eyes to Fargo.

"You can lock these robbin' bushwhackers up," Fargo said, and the man looked uncomfortable as he glanced at Ma Cowley again.

"What for?" he asked, and Fargo quickly told him what had happened. When he finished, the deputy glanced at Ma Cowley again and the discomfort was clear in the grimace he offered.

"I only have two cells," the deputy said.

"That's enough," Fargo said.

"He's lyin'," Ma Cowley interrupted. "That whole story's a crock of shit."

The deputy looked at her and something close to hope came into his face, Fargo saw in astonishment. "It is?" the man said.

"He made it up to get back at me because I wouldn't let him take that little girl to bed," the huge woman said with a sweep of righteousness.

"Goddamn, she's the one that's lying," Fargo said. "Where's the sheriff?"

"He left," the man said.

"When?" Fargo frowned.

"Two months ago," the deputy said. "Town's never put on a new sheriff."

Fargo glanced at Ma Cowley and swore silently. A smug curl of triumph touched her wide mouth. "Lock them up. I'll sign the charges," Fargo almost shouted.

"You can't do that. He's lyin', made it all up, I told you. Right, boys?" Ma Cowley said.

"That's right," Zeb agreed.

"Right," Zane echoed.

Fargo's eyes went to Cassie. She said nothing and her nod was almost imperceptible. He saw the deputy shrug his shoulders apologetically.

"It's four against one," the lawman muttered.

Fargo fumed and his eyes shot to the huge woman again. The deputy didn't want to jail anyone and it was plain she'd known as much. "Tell him to give me back my rifle," the woman barked to the deputy, and Fargo turned his gaze on the man, his eyes cold as a lake in midwinter.

"Walk," he growled, and the man half-shrugged again, turned, and hurried away. Fargo stared at Ma Cowley. "I'll see you four again and you won't need a jail," he said.

The huge woman's eyes held defiance. "Give me my rifle back," she said.

Fargo threw the big Hawkens on the ground, drew his Colt, and fired a single shot that blasted the rifle's loading chamber into a gaping hole of torn and twisted metal. With a curse of anger and frustration, he swung the Ovaro around and galloped away. He knew a dead end when he saw one, and Ma Cowley and her tribe weren't worth more of his time. Somebody else would have to put a stop to their robbing little schemes.

He turned the Ovaro north and rode toward Beaverhead in Montana Territory. He put the strange interruption behind him but allowed himself to wonder what little Cassie might have been like had she not been playing bait.

When the night descended, he found a place to bed down and slept soundly and quickly until the morning woke him with its warm sun. A refreshing stream and a bush of wild cherries provided breakfast before he rode west, picked up the Madison River, and followed its weaving course into Beaverhead and beyond.

Four clusters of wagons had set up camp beside the river at what was plainly a staging area. Fargo halted beside the first two, a converted hay wagon and an Owensboro huckster rig with high sides.

A man stepped forward from beside a woman and three children. "Looking for somebody?" he asked.

"Abel Gunnard," Fargo said.

"I believe he's with the last wagons along the bank," the man said.

With a nod, Fargo walked the Ovaro forward. He came to four wagons grouped in a half-circle, two Conestogas and two big California rack-beds equipped with top bows and good canvas covering. A half-dozen yards away he saw ten horses tethered in a line, their riders lounging beside the river. A man swung down from the rear of the first California rack-bed. He was of medium height, with brown hair thinning on top, and a sharp-nosed face with quick, shrewd eyes. There was no hint of weakness in the face, but only a mean, uncaring cast to it.

"Looking for Abel Gunnard," Fargo said.

"You found him," the man answered.

"I'm Fargo," the Trailsman said, and Abel Gunnard's eyes widened at once.

"Welcome, Fargo. Been waiting for you. I was afraid maybe you didn't get the last letter I sent you."

"I got it and I'm here but I'm having second thoughts, Gunnard," Fargo said. "You've pushed this trip back twice since I got that first payment voucher."

"Unfortunate delays," Abel Gunnard said.

"Winter's looking down your throat now. You've no time left to cross the Bitterroot range. Same for trying to go around the long way," Fargo said.

"We can make it. There's a way," Abel Gunnard said. "We'll talk about it tonight."

Fargo shrugged and nodded toward the cowhands beside the river. "They with you?" he asked, and the man nodded. Fargo's glance went to the two Conestogas at the other side of the half-circle. "You said there'd be five wagons."

"One more to come. I expect it'll be here today or tomorrow," Gunnard said. "Let me introduce you to the rest of the folks coming along." He started toward the first Conestoga and Fargo felt surprise stab at him as Hope Maxwell swung down from the tail of the wagon, shoulder-length brown hair framing her round brown eyes and round cheeks.

"I'll be dammed," Fargo murmured as she smiled at him.

"You were right. The world is full of coincidences," she said.

"You two know each other?" Abel Gunnard frowned.

"Let's say we've met," she answered, her eyes locked with Fargo's.

"This is Skye Fargo, the Trailsman," Gunnard introduced.

"And he's as good-looking with clothes as without them." The young woman smiled.

"Sounds like you *do* know each other," Abel Gunnard commented.

"Sounds better than it was. But it was a good deed, in any case," Fargo said. "Tell you about it sometime." He reached into his saddlebag and brought out the clothes Hope had given him. "Thanks, again," he said. "They came in right handy." His glance shifted to the second Conestoga as a woman stepped out with two small boys about six and seven years old.

"This is Vera Maxwell, my brother's wife," Hope Maxwell introduced. "And Ted and Tim."

"Hello," Fargo said as he took in the woman's slender figure and drawn, wan face; it had undoubtedly once been lovely, but was now empty and full of pain. She looked back with her haunted blue eyes.

"You going to take us to our daddy?" the one little boy asked.

"Maybe," Fargo said.

Both youngsters looked very much alike, both with small, pug noses and round faces, but one had short brown hair, the other blond hair that grew longer. Without uttering a word, Vera Maxwell returned to her wagon, but the two boys skipped their way toward the riverbank.

"Don't get your feet wet," Hope called after them.

"Come over and meet my foreman," Gunnard said, and led Fargo to where the ten cowhands lounged. A good-sized man with a strong jaw and a handshake to match came forward. "Gabe Hazzard," Gunnard introduced.

"Glad to meet you, Fargo. Heard about you often enough," the man said.

"Nothing bad, I hope." Fargo grinned.

"Only that you're the best, and we'll be needing that," Hazzard said.

Abel Gunnard led Fargo away, back to the first rack-bed wagon where a woman emerged, a brassy blonde. Her tight little curls were a color that came out of a bottle, and she wore too much lipstick and a half-pout. But her eyes were bright, quickly appraising, and Fargo decided she was pretty in a hard way. Her demure blouse and skirt didn't fit the rest of her and he smiled, certain the outfit had been Abel Gunnard's doing.

"Harriet," Gunnard said. "We're partners."

Fargo accepted the description without comment and Gunnard shifted uneasily on one foot. "Why don't you unsaddle your horse and settle in, Fargo?" the man said. "Supper will be ready soon, lamb stew from last night. Always better the second night. Then we'll talk."

Fargo agreed with a nod, walked to the Ovaro, and removed the horse's saddle as dusk slid over the land. He used the dandy brush to give the horse a quick grooming.

Gunnard's men had a fire going and two kettles of stew on the flame by the time darkness fell. He moved to the fire after the others had gathered themselves around the flame, Gunnard's hired hands grouped pretty much to themselves. Fargo sat down near Hope Maxwell and across from Vera and the two boys. He took a tin plate of the stew and found the meal tasty.

"Eb Story's the best cook west of the Mississippi," Abel Gunnard said as he set his empty plate aside. "Now, about the trip, Fargo. There's one way we can cross the Bitterroot range before the snows come, and that's going through Blood Pass. I've seen old fur-trappers' maps. They mark it as the only pass that cuts right across the center of the range."

"That's likely so," Fargo said.

"We can go through most of the pass, across the top and far enough onto the other side to set up camp for the winter," Gunnard said.

Fargo glanced at the men as they finished their meals, handed in their plates, and began to drift away. Gunnard had hired them with good money and assurances of a hard but safe venture, Fargo was certain, maybe with the promise of bonuses. He didn't want to strike at the man's authority or honesty, so he decided to wait until the men had left. He watched Vera Maxwell collect the plates from the two boys and turn them over to the cook.

"I'll be putting the boys and myself to bed now," she said. "Good night."

Fargo's eyes followed her as she shepherded Ted and Tim to the Conestoga. He had yet to see the woman's drawn face smile, he reflected. When the last of the men had returned to the riverbank to bed down, he fixed Abel Gunnard with a hard stare.

"You've some special reason for wanting to go through Blood Pass," he said.

"I told you, it seems to be the only way through the center of the range," the man answered.

"There's more. Let's have it," Fargo said.

Gunnard smiled slowly. "You're a sharp man, Fargo. But I knew that much," he said. "That's what makes you the best. That second rack-bed over there is loaded with digging tools. An old prospector made a map of the way mineral veins run through a section of earth. He's convinced me that there's a fortune in precious minerals—emerald, sapphire, jade, agate, even diamonds—at the foot of the far side of Blood Pass. I aim to get that fortune."

Fargo nodded, his face still grave, and turned his gaze on Hope Maxwell. "My brother crossed Blood Pass over a year ago. Nobody's heard from him since. Vera has become a shell, a woman wasting away. I'm sure you saw that," she said.

"I did." Fargo nodded.

"Our doctor back in Utah agreed that the only thing that will help her is to find out what's happened to her husband. It's become an obsession with her. She's convinced he's alive and well and somehow his letters have been lost. I agreed to go along with her—one, to help with the boys, and two, because my brother and I were very close," Hope said.

"What was he doing in Blood Pass?" Fargo asked.

"He'd been hired by a man named O'Dell to find a mail route through the Bitterroot range that would cut months from the time it takes the post to reach California now," she said, and Fargo stared out at the night for a moment before returning his gaze to her and Abel Gunnard. He chose Gunnard first and heard the hardness come into his voice.

"You know why it's called Blood Pass?" he asked.

"A name." Gunnard shrugged. "Lots of funny names out here."

"It's called that because that's all anyone has ever left there . . . their blood," Fargo said grimly. "And that's all you'll leave there. First, you're wrong about having time to make the other side before the snows come. You'll be trapped by blizzards the likes of which you've never imagined. You won't have the time to build shelters and settle in, not starting this late. But then it's not likely you'll have to worry about the snows."

"Meaning what?" Gunnard asked.

"Meaning the mountains have a lot of ways of killing, and if they don't do you in, there's the Nez Percé. You can count on their doing it," Fargo said.

Gunnard's smile was sly. "That's one of the reasons I hired you, Fargo. I heard you know the chief of the Bitterroot Nez Percé. I figure you can use your friendship to get him to back off," the man said.

"You figured wrong, Gunnard," Fargo said. "I know Walking Deer, but that won't mean steer shit in getting you through Blood Pass. There's a Nez Percé burial ground at the top. That's sacred ground. Only the Nez Percé can step on that ground without contaminating it. Any outsider who sets foot on it must be killed. And they'll do it with pleasure and with hate."

"I'm not letting some damn-fool Indian taboo keep me from a fortune in precious stones, Fargo," Abel Gunnard said. "And you're not backing out on me."

"I agreed to break trail, not commit suicide," Fargo said.

"You owe me. I'd have started a month ago except you took a job with Ansel Gray," Gunnard shot back.

"That's twisting things. I took Ansel's job because you'd put your start off twice," Fargo returned.

"It still put me back one more month," Gunnard said. "And you took the money voucher I sent you. That means you made a deal, Fargo. I always heard you weren't the kind to back out on your word. I expect you to keep your agreement now." He strode away and disappeared into his wagon, satisfied that he'd made his point. He had, even though it was twisted to suit himself, Fargo grunted. He wouldn't back out of the bargain, not yet. That wasn't his way, as the man had been quick to point out. He'd try to let Abel Gunnard see the truth of his wrongheaded decision in other ways before he turned back.

He gazed at Hope Maxwell. Maybe she could be a start, he thought as he noticed her studying him.

"I'm waiting," she said. "I'm sure you've words for me."

"Bull's-eye," Fargo grunted. "Gunnard's got an old map, old miner's talk and greed. That can make a man desert his senses. All you have is the thin thread of hope."

"I've got more," she said. "And something that makes you wrong about some of what you just told Abel Gunnard." His brows lifted and she reached into the pocket of her skirt and drew out a letter. She leaned toward the last of the firelight. "It's from my brother to Vera and I'll read only the part that's important to us," she said. " 'My dear wife . . . I have crossed over the top of Blood Pass and have started down the other side. But I have stopped and built a lean-to so's I'll have a place to rest when I come back this way. Give my love to the boys. I will return before you know it.' " She halted, straightened, and put the letter back into her pocket as she looked at Fargo.

"Only there was never another letter and he never came back," Fargo ventured.

"That's right, but don't you see what else it means?" Hope asked. "He crossed that sacred burial ground and lived. He had started down the other side and built himself a lean-to."

"That doesn't mean whit," Fargo said harshly.

"It means an outsider can cross over the top of the pass and live," Hope countered.

"It means maybe he got lucky and made it across. It also means he paid for it," Fargo said.

"You don't know that," she protested.

"The hell I don't," he said sourly. "How'd Vera get that letter?"

"He had taken a helper with him, a young boy

40

named Jack Dowd. His body was found last spring on the banks of the Bitterroot River. They figured it had been washed down by the spring thaw because it was still frozen stiff. The letter was in his pocket," Hope explained. "Don't you see, Tom had sent him back with the letter, but he met with an accident along the way."

"He met with the Nez Percé," Fargo growled.

"You can't be sure of that. It could've been a simple accident," she insisted.

"Christ, your brother's had a year to come back. Doesn't that say anything to you, girl?" Fargo pushed at her. He saw the refusal flash in her eyes, but there was pain inside the anger.

"It says maybe he's hurt somewhere. Maybe he's lying in a town on the other side of the mountains with his memory gone. Those things happen, you know. Maybe all he needs is for someone to find him," she said. "You don't know how to hope, Fargo."

"You don't know how to face truth, honey," he said with more sadness than anger.

Her lips tightened as she looked away. "Vera has to know," she murmured.

"And kill herself for it?" Fargo speared.

"She's dying this way," Hope said.

"And the boys?" he pressed.

"I didn't want her to bring the boys, but there was no place to leave them—no relatives, no one," Hope said.

"Go back now. He's dead," Fargo said, and knew he was being no more harsh than truthful. But Hope shook her head slowly.

"Not now. Vera wouldn't. She paid her way, came all the way out here. She's not turning back now," Hope said. "Maybe if all the things you say are right, I'll get her to turn back."

"Hell, there's no turning back when it's too late," Fargo snapped, and her shrug was a combination of helplessness and resignation. She rose, the round, brown eyes sad.

"I'm going to turn in," she said. "I hope you'll take us through. I know you're the best."

"And if I don't?" he asked.

She shrugged again. "We have to try," she said, and walked away.

He waited as she vanished into the darkness. "Damn," he bit out, and took his bedroll to one side. She was too pretty to have her head hanging on a Nez Percé lance.

He set out his bedroll, undressed, and stared out at the dark outline of the towering mountains. In their dark beauty lay anguish and death. Maybe he could make Hope Maxwell realize that before time ran out. She had extended a helping hand when he needed it. He could do no less for her, and maybe Abel Gunnard would come to his senses.

There was a fifth wagon still due, he reminded himself. Maybe they'd bring some reason along and listen to him. He closed his eyes.

3

When morning came, Fargo rose early, washed, re-filled his canteen at the river's edge, and took a tin cup of good hot coffee Eb Story had brewed.

Ted and Tim scampered from their Conestoga to halt beside him. "We going to start today, Fargo?" the one with the brown hair said.

"Hope so. You Tim?" Fargo asked.

"I'm Ted. He's Tim," the boy said, and pointed to his brother's longer, blond hair.

"Got it now," Fargo said.

"Can we ride with you, Fargo? We've got our po-nies with us," Tim asked hopefully.

"Maybe. We'll find a time, I'm sure," Fargo said, and glanced at Vera Maxwell as she stepped from the wagon and walked past him carrying an empty bucket, her drawn face set, her eyes downcast. She went to the river and filled the bucket. Fargo peered over to the other Conestoga as Hope stepped down. She wore a black skirt and a white shirt that pulled taut around the round fullness of her breasts.

" 'Morning," she said with firm politeness. The morn-ing sun accentuated the prettiness of her face, but he saw the determination still in her eyes. She accepted a cup of coffee from the cook and Fargo saw Abel Gunnard emerge from his California rack-bed, fol-lowed by the brassy blonde Harriet. Her rounded, busty figure again demurely clothed in a high-buttoned blouse and full skirt made Fargo smile. They took their coffees and Harriet followed, sipping hers, as Gunnard came up to him.

43

"You done your thinking, Fargo?" the man asked.

"I'll go on for a spell," Fargo said. "So's I can get you back when you come to your senses."

Gunnard nodded, but there was satisfaction in his face and he strolled away. Fargo saw Hope looking on and Harriet stepped closer to him, her voice low, confidential. "Abel told me about the way you feel," she said. "You putting it on extra thick so's he'll call it off?"

"I wish that was it," Fargo said. Her eyes stayed on him, thoughtful, searching. "What makes you want to get yourself killed?" he asked crudely.

"I'm not here to do that," Harriet said. "I'm here because Abel wants me here." Her hardness suddenly softened and the half-pout dropped from her lips. "Abel's been real good to me for a long time, better than anyone ever has. I'll do whatever he wants, go wherever he goes, face whatever he faces."

"That love or gratitude?" Fargo asked.

"Maybe both. Call it whatever you want. But I'm here with him and for him," Harriet said. "You don't know Abel. He's a good man who's always had to fight his way through life. Now he feels he has the big chance he's always wanted."

"The big chance to be killed," Fargo snorted.

Harriet shrugged, her face grave, and walked away, still sipping her coffee. Under the bottle-blond hair and all the brassbound hardness, Harriet had come to an accommodation with herself and he gave her credit for that. It was more than many did. He felt bitter as he thought of how she might die with that accommodation. He slowed as Hope came over to cross his path, disapproval in her face.

"I heard what you said to Abel about taking us partway," she said, the sentence filled with the unsaid.

"Go on," he grunted.

"I don't think much of it," she sniffed. "I don't like halfway things, halfway commitments, halfway promises."

"Half a loaf's better than none," Fargo snapped.

"Not always. Halfway interest means a halfway effort," she returned coldly.

Fargo felt anger stab into him at her disdainful stand. "You play with words, honey. I'll tend to what's real," he said, and strode away from her. He went to where he'd tethered the Ovaro and took the time to give the magnificent black-and-white horse a quick grooming. He was using the hoof pick to clean out trail crud when he noticed the sun had gone past the noon sky.

Abel Gunnard and Harriet returned from the river-bank with a basket of newly washed clothes, and some of the hired hands were playing with Ted and Tim. Fargo finished with the Ovaro and had just put his gear away when he saw the wagon approaching, a high-sided Studebaker farm wagon with a canvas-top cover.

"Looks like our fifth wagon has arrived," Abel Gunnard said as the wagon continued toward them, three riders alongside. But Fargo only half-heard the man's voice as he stared at the huge figure driving, mountainous breasts shaking under the loose black tent of a dress. His glance paused at the thin, blond figure and the other two fat forms riding along.

"No," Fargo heard himself mutter. "No goddamn way." He stayed in place as the wagon pulled to a halt in front of Abel.

"This the Gunnard train?" the woman asked.

Abel nodded. "You must be Ma Cowley," he said. "Been waiting for you."

"Had some delays," the woman said in her rasping bellow. "These are my boys, Zeb and Zane. And that's Cassie. We're all set to roll."

Fargo stepped forward from behind the Ovaro and enjoyed the astonishment that flooded the huge woman's wide face.

"What in hell's he doing here?" Ma blurted.

"This is Skye Fargo . . . the Trailsman. He's going to break trail for us through the pass."

"No he isn't," Fargo bit out, and saw Gunnard's glance of astonishment. "Not if that pack of thievin' jackals goes along."

He watched a whirlwind of thoughts race through the huge woman's small eyes and saw her gather herself in with cunning self-discipline. "Now, look here, Fargo, you don't want to go holding a grudge, do you?" she slid out at him.

"I sure as hell do," Fargo growled.

"This is why we needed the money," she said with almost righteous reasonableness. "We had to get us a new wagon. That old one was plumb wore out. You saw that."

Fargo turned his eyes on Gunnard, who still looked on with wide-eyed surprise. Hope and Vera had come out of their wagons. "They go and I don't," he said. "It's as simple as that. Your choice."

Gunnard frowned at the icy anger he saw in the big man's lake-blue eyes. "You really mean that, don't you?" he murmured.

"For damn sure," Fargo snapped. "They're a thieving pack of bushwhackers. They're no damn good and they'll only bring you trouble."

Abel Gunnard turned back to Ma Cowley and his shoulders lifted in resignation. "Sorry, but I need a trailsman more than another wagon," he said.

"You can't do this, goddammit," the huge woman roared. "I paid you fifty dollars in advance."

Gunnard pulled a roll of bills from his pocket, peeled off five, and handed them up to the woman. "Here's your money back," he said. "I'm sorry."

"I don't want the damn money. I want to cross those mountains," Ma Cowley raged.

Gunnard kept his hand stretched out with the money in it. "The man gave me a choice and I made it," he said. "You can hook up with another train."

Ma Cowley snatched the money from Gunnard's hand, but her eyes went to Fargo, small agates of fury. "You cowshit bastard. You'll be sorry for this," she snarled.

"Not so's you'll notice," Fargo said blandly.

"Let me shoot him. I owe him, Ma," Zeb's voice cut in.

Fargo's eyes flicked to the paunchy figure and his arms automatically tensed.

"Shut up, Zeb," Ma Cowley snapped. "That's just what he'd like you to try."

Fargo let a tight smile edge his lips. "Ma gets the cigar," he growled.

"Bastard," the woman rasped. "You can't stop me from crossing Blood Pass. It's a free country. I'll just follow along."

"I can't stop you from going your way, but you're not dogging my trail. You stay far enough away so's I don't see you. I catch sight of any of you, I'll come down shooting, you hear me, lard ass?" Fargo said.

Ma Cowley's small eyes were pinpoints of hate. "I hear you," she muttered, snapping the reins over her team and turning the wagon around. The others followed but Fargo caught Cassie's glance at him, almost a hint of apology in it.

"I don't have to ask," he heard Hope say and saw the faintly sardonic smile on her lips.

"You don't," he grunted sourly.

"I hope the little blonde looks a lot better with her clothes off; she sure doesn't look like much with them on," Hope tossed out.

"She does," Fargo said, and cursed himself for sounding defensive.

"Some men think anything naked looks good," Hope said waspishly, and hurried away before he could throw back even a glower.

Abel Gunnard moved closer. "We've a few hours of good light left. No sense wasting it, especially as you feel time's so important," he said. "We can roll now."

"I want to look at each wagon first," Fargo said, and Gunnard agreed with a nod.

"You can start with mine," he said, and led Fargo to the first rack-bed. Inside, Harriet sat on a mattress and Fargo saw the wagon filled with household things, clothing trunks, two rifles, assorted boxes, and a concertina, which drew a smile from him. "Harriet plays it," Gunnard said. "Real well, too."

"Hope to hear her do so," Fargo said, and went on to the next rack-bed, and his eyes hardened at once as Gunnard let him look inside. The wagon, heavy-axled as it was, was overloaded with shovels, axes, pickaxes, rakes, long lengths of cut planking for shoring timber, heavy saws, and every variety of tool, including an iron winch. "Too much," Fargo grunted. "Way overloaded."

"I've got the strongest horses hitched to it. They've had no trouble so far," Gunnard said.

"They haven't been in mountain country," Fargo said.

"I'll need every bit of this gear," Gunnard insisted, and Fargo shrugged.

"It's overloaded. You won't make it in mountain country," Fargo said. "Put some of it into your other wagon."

"Harriet won't ride with a wagonful of shovels and planking," Gunnard complained.

"That's your problem. I've said my piece," Fargo answered, and moved on to Vera's Conestoga. The inside was as neat as any proper living room, with a small mattress for each of the boys facing each other. He saw a number of the hatboxes that had been in Hope's wagon and an open trunk filled with men's clothes. "Obliged," he said, and backed from the wagon to see Hope waiting beside her Conestoga. "No need," he said. "I've seen inside your wagon." Her brows knitted in an instant frown. "You were asleep," he said, and enjoyed the twin dots of color that appeared in her round cheeks.

"I'll get the men ready to ride," Gunnard said. "Maybe I can shift some things into my wagon when the time comes." Fargo nodded and strode to the Ovaro. Chances were Gunnard would get around to lightening his supply wagon when it was too late, Fargo snorted, pausing to tighten the cinch on the Ovaro before swinging up on the horse.

He took the pinto past the wagons and rode ahead to where Blood Pass began as a wide passageway through the foothills. It stayed that way with a gentle slope, wound through terrain lush with hackberry, cottonwood, oak, and ironwood. The air stayed brisk, signaling an end to Indian summer, and Fargo rode on with an easy pace, scanned the good, thick terrain that rose up on both sides of the passage, and as dusk began to descend, he halted at a place where the road widened.

He had the Ovaro tethered and unsaddled and a fire started when the others arrived. Gunnard's men riding in first.

"Mighty welcome sight, that fire," Gabe Hazzard said.

"Much obliged," Eb Story chimed in. "Now all I have to do is get to cooking." He was quick about his task, Fargo saw, and was dishing out plates of beans and pork soon after darkness descended.

Hope appeared and Fargo watched her settle down near him with her plate. "We in Blood Pass?" she asked.

"Been in it for the last few hours," he answered.

"Hardly seems so formidable as you make it out to be," she said.

"Blood Pass is a woman who seems easy to get along with at first but soon turns into a witch," Fargo said.

"What an interesting way to put it," Hope said.

"I thought so," Fargo said. "And just for your information, honey, I don't think everything naked looks good. Truth is, I think most women look better with their clothes on than off. You'd most likely be included."

"That's a rotten thing to say. You're just striking back. You're angry because I didn't think much of what you got yourself bushwhacked for," she said, and added a smug little laugh.

Damn her hide, he muttered silently. She was half-right but he wasn't about to tell her so. "I just thought maybe you were different than most," he said. "But you're not."

"Different how?" Hope frowned.

"Smarter. Wiser. Less bitchy. Able to understand about beauty," he pushed at her.

"Understand what exactly?" she pressed.

"That it doesn't come in one shape or one color or one size. A rose is rich and full and shimmers and is beautiful for being that. A lily of the valley is delicate and slender and fragile and has its own kind of beauty," he said.

She peered at him for a moment, a furrow dug into her smooth forehead. "That's either a very sensitive attitude or the best excuse for screwing every woman you can," she said.

"Or both." Fargo laughed.

She rose, took her plate, and strode away, her back held very straight. But he noticed that her hips and her hair swung in rhythmic unison.

He rose, turned in his plate, and carried his bedroll off to the side of the camp. He settled in under the low branches of a wide tanbark oak and slept quickly. Every night of sound sleep was to be savored, he knew. There'd be too many of a different kind lying ahead.

He slept until the morning sun crept through the branches and woke, washed, dressed quickly, and had the Ovaro saddled while the camp stirred into waking. He waited for Eb Story to brew a pot of coffee, downed the bracing liquid, and sent the Ovaro up into the passageway speckled by the morning sun.

The foothills presented little danger, he realized, but his eyes swept the terrain out of habit and he slowed when he saw a line of unshod hoofprints cross the road. Two Indian ponies, he read, moving slowly, at least twenty-four hours ago. He moved the Ovaro forward at the same easy pace and turned when he heard the sound of hoofbeats following. His hand rested on the butt of the big Colt at his side as the two ponies came into view, a small rider atop each.

"Hi, Fargo," Tim called, his blond hair catching a ray of sunlight.

Fargo frowned at both boys as they came up beside him. "Who knows you're here?" he asked.

"Nobody. Ma saw us take our ponies but she thinks we're riding along behind," Ted said.

"We went into the trees and rode past everyone," Tim added proudly.

Fargo's face remained stern. "That's the last time," he said.

"Last time for what?" Ted asked.

"For that kind of stunt," Fargo snapped. "You don't go anywhere anytime without permission from now on. The same's going to go for everybody else."

"You said we could ride with you," Tim countered with a half-pout.

"I said maybe, and I expected you'd be asking first," Fargo said, and remained stern-faced. Both their young, unlined faces grew solemn. "Everybody's entitled to one mistake, only out here sometimes that's your last one," Fargo said. "You're here, so you might as well ride along a spell."

Both their faces broke into instant joy and they swung their ponies on both sides of the pinto. "You see any Indians, yet?" Tim asked.

"No, but they're around," Fargo said.

"Hope said you're going to help find our pa for us," Ted remarked.

Fargo swore silently. "I'll try," he said.

"I hope you can do it. Maybe it'll make Ma be the way she used to be. She never laughs anymore," Ted said, and Fargo swore again under his breath. Trust and innocence, he bit out silently. The gifts of the young. The world would rob them of that all too quickly. He'd not hurry it along any faster, even though they deserved better than the hollowness of false hopes.

"Show me what you boys know about tracking," he said, eager to change the subject. The boys were eagerly proud to confide what little they knew. He let them ride along with him for another hour until he halted at a stream and waited for the wagons to catch up.

Gabe Hazzard and his crew arrived first, but Fargo said nothing until everyone was halted at the stream. "Ted and Tim have agreed they won't go off riding without getting my permission," he said. "That goes for everybody else, too. You'll stay together unless you come see me first."

"I don't take to being treated like a kid, mister," a voice said, and Fargo saw a man with a stubbled face and a defensive arrogance in his eyes.

"I don't take to it, either," the man beside him said, taller, with a long face that held the shadow of truculence in it.

"What's your name?" Fargo asked the first man.

"Akins," the man said. Fargo's glance went to the taller one.

"Simpson," the man said.

"I don't want to treat anybody like kids, but I know these mountains and I know the Indians. I gave an order and I expect it to be followed," Fargo said.

"You break trail, mister. That's your job. I ride where and when I want," Akins said doggedly, and Fargo turned away. He didn't want ugly scenes, not yet, and he waited for the rest of the men to return to their saddles before he paused beside Gabe Hazzard.

"You're the foreman. See that they follow orders," he said.

"They're men, Fargo, experienced hands. You can't treat them like that."

"None of them are Indian fighters, not even on the plains. Up here they might as well be kids. See that they stay in line," Fargo said.

"I can't promise they'll take that kind of order," Hazzard said, and Fargo rode away with a glance at Abel Gunnard, who watched from his wagon.

Fargo rode on up the steepening passage and slowed when he heard a horse following in a hurry. Hope appeared on a thin-legged brown gelding and came up beside him.

"Thought I'd ride along with you," she said.

"Ask next time," he growled.

"May I ride along?" she said with cool formality. "I have Eb Story driving my rig."

"For a spell," he said.

"The boys enjoyed their ride with you," she commented.

"I'll thank you not to go telling them I'm going to find their pa for them," Fargo said.

"That bother you?" she asked blandly.

"Any dumb thing bothers me," he grunted.

"The boys need a man's presence. That's another reason it's so important Vera know one way or the other. She has to come to terms with herself and settle down to a new life. Or pick up the old one. But she can't without knowing. The pain's too deep inside her," Hope said, and Fargo rode on without comment. "You change your mind about only taking us so far?" Hope questioned, trying to sound casual.

"Nope," Fargo said. "Something make you think I would?"

"I thought maybe talking to the boys might make you see things differently," she answered.

"It made me wish I could wave a magic wand and send you all the hell back to town," Fargo snapped.

"Then I guess there's nothing more to be said on that subject," she remarked coolly.

"Guess not," he agreed, and slowed as the trail suddenly split into two sections, one higher than the other. "Blood Pass does this often," he muttered. "We take the high path. They'll follow our prints."

"Why the high one?" Hope queried.

"It'll be drier, firmer. Rainwater will settle into the lower one and stay there longer," Fargo said.

She nodded and seemed to take mental note of what he'd said. Later, when the paths converged again, she asked why he halted beside a pair of tall bur oaks.

"See the grass around the base of each tree. It's dry, turning brown," Fargo said.

"Sign of winter coming on," she said.

"No, a sign that it's been very dry for some while," he said. "That means the pass will be dry and hard."

"Better dry than wet," she said.

"Not always," he said, and spurred the Ovaro on. He felt her eyes on him as he scanned the land and she asked questions whenever he halted. "You always this inquisitive?" he said finally.

"I like knowing things," she said.

He nodded but a smile curled inside him. He rode on and pointed out a hackberry that leaned precariously toward the pass. "I'll have Gunnard's men cut that down before the wagons cross by it," he said.

"It's probably been hanging like that for years," she said.

"Not with the vibration of four heavy wagons passing by. The ground's very dry, remember, and dry ground doesn't give a tree much support. We'll wait here," he said, and dismounted.

"It's obvious that you're everything they say you are," Hope said, folding herself down beside him. "But it's not all as deadly as you've made it out to be," she said, and he frowned at her. "Blood Pass, I mean," she went on. "You know it. You've gone through Blood Pass and you're still alive. You're proof it can be done."

"I've never gone through Blood Pass," Fargo corrected. "I've never crossed the sacred burial grounds, and maybe that's why I'm alive. I've only gone far enough to meet with Walking Deer." Hope peered at him. "Sorry to disappoint you, honey," he said, and she fell silent until the first of the wagons appeared.

Fargo waved Gabe Hazzard to him, but the man had already taken in the tree and quickly barked orders to his crew. Six pulled long-bladed two-man saws from the supply wagon and sent the tree crashing to the road in minutes. They cut it into manageable pieces and pulled them aside.

"They're quick and efficient," Hope commented.

"Too bad they won't have a chance to show what they can really do," Fargo murmured, and saw Hope fix him with a faintly amused gaze.

"You can stop all your negative, sour remarks," she

said. "They're not going to work. We're all going to push on."

"They say misery loves company. So does stupidity, I guess," he snapped, and pulled himself onto the Ovaro.

"I'd still like to ride along," she said.

"Suit yourself," he said, and sent the Ovaro into a trot.

She caught up to him moments later and fell into step alongside. Again he saw her watching his every move, the way he peered at things close and things far away. But she'd pulled back on pushing questions at him and he cracked a wry smile.

When the afternoon began to slip toward sunset, he turned to her as the wind whipped sharply down from the high peaks. "Learn enough?" he asked, and saw the surprise flash in her round brown eyes for an instant.

"I just like to observe things," she said, recovering quickly.

"I see." He nodded. "You observe that wind sweeping down? That's a message."

"Wind isn't snow," Hope said.

"No, but it tells you what to expect when the sky turns gray," Fargo said. "You observe anything else?" he asked.

"Such as?" she answered warily.

"Indian pony prints. Piece of a Blackfoot moccasin off to the side of the trail. Riders in the deep tree cover to our left," he said, and she stared at him and swallowed hard.

"I'm new at this. I can't be expected to see what you see," she returned defensively.

He said nothing more and sent the Ovaro up a steep and narrow pathway that led away from the main pass. When he reached the top, he halted and watched Hope's gelding follow with a good deal of effort, the horse not rugged enough to handle real hard mountain riding. But Hope managed to bring him to the top, where he rested, breathing hard.

Fargo's gaze scanned the terrain below and to the rear. The wagons came into view, vanished behind a cluster of trees, and reappeared again. But Fargo's gaze stayed in the distance to their rear.

"You really think they're following?" Hope frowned.

"I think Ma Cowley's desperate enough, stupid enough, and mean enough," Fargo said. "But if she's following she's staying back plenty far, and that's all I care about." He turned the pinto and carefully negotiated the steep passage down to the main train and heard Hope's mount slipping and stumbling after him.

The day began to drift toward an end and the wind grew sharper when he found a half-circle of space and walked the pinto into it. Dusk still held off as the wagons arrived and Gabe Hazzard approached him.

"Akins and Simpson want to go shoot us some jackrabbit for dinner," the foreman said.

"Cook got enough on hand for supper?" Fargo asked.

"Beans and pork chitlins," the man said. "But the boys would all enjoy fresh rabbit."

"No rabbit," Fargo said. "Tell Akins and Simpson they stay in camp."

Gabe Hazzard's face reflected disappointment and disagreement as he strode away, and Fargo took his bedroll off into the brush. He returned when night fell and sat down near the fire with a plate of beans and pork strips and found Ted and Tim beside him.

"Can we ride with you some tomorrow, Fargo?" Tim asked.

"You can show us how to track an Indian, or maybe a bear," Ted chimed in.

"Most times you can't track an Indian." Fargo laughed. "And most times you don't need to track a bear. You can smell him." He tousled Tim's hair and saw the youngster revel in his touch. "You can ride some with me in the morning, but I want somebody else along," he said.

"To take the boys back in a hurry if need be, I assume," Hope said, and Fargo nodded. "I'll go along," she said.

"I was thinking of Gabe Hazzard or one of his men," Fargo said, and saw her bristle at once.

"The boys are my responsibility, mine and Vera's. I'll go along," she said. "I assure you I can run as fast as anyone with them," she added sarcastically, and Vera came over, motioning to Ted and Tim. They rose at once.

"G'night, Fargo," Ted said.

"See you in the morning," Tim added as they hurried off after Vera.

"She ever say anything?" Fargo asked Hope.

"When we're alone," Hope answered, and shivered as a sudden stab of wind swept over the fire, which was hardly more than embers now.

"It's nice and warm in my bedroll," Fargo remarked idly.

She turned a coolly aloof gaze at him. "I suppose directness is a form of charm with some women," she said.

He shrugged. "Nothing ventured, nothing gained."

She rose, paused a moment more, and a tiny smile laced the question. "If I said yes, would it change your mind about staying on?"

"No," he answered honestly.

"I didn't think so," she murmured smugly.

"If I said yes, would you come?" he tossed back.

"No," she answered.

"Didn't think so." He grinned and watched her walk away with purposeful slowness, giving her hips an added swing that was her own last word. He smiled as he rose; he went to his bedroll and undressed, then crawled into its warmth. Hope Maxwell had shown she could be acute, understanding, bitchy, clever, and determined. They were all good signs. He just had to find how to make them all come together in the right way. He could, he was certain, if he had time. Sourness swept over him instantly. There wouldn't be time, not on this venture. He closed his eyes, shut away further thoughts, and slept.

Morning came with the air cold and crisp but the

sun still bright, and Fargo was grateful for the coffee Eb Story had ready. Ted and Tim appeared leading their ponies before anyone else woke and Fargo laughed at their bright-eyed eagerness as he silently cursed their being there. Hope emerged from her Conestoga in Levi's that clung to a very round rear, he noted, and a blue shirt that hung softly on full, round breasts that showed not the faintest outline of a tiny point. She drank the coffee Eb Story gave her and returned on the thin-legged gelding.

Fargo saddled the pinto and led the way up the pass as Abel Gunnard and Harriet emerged arm in arm from their wagon. He slowed to a pace that the boys' ponies could take, and the cold air swept through the narrow places with biting glee. His lake-blue eyes scanned the high land on both sides and ahead as they rode. Ted and Tim were bundles of high-pitched excitement when he halted and pointed out where Indian ponies had gathered for the night. A piece of broken arrow shaft provided an extra excuse for excited squeals and Ted put the piece of shaft into his belt as they rode on.

Hope, Fargo noted, searched the hills as he did, and he smiled to himself. But she had stayed in the background and let the boys have him all to themselves.

Blood Pass continued its steady climb and Fargo saw that they were beginning to reach the start of the middle range, so he called a halt where the trail leveled off for a few hundred yards. They had ridden most of the morning, the boys enjoying every minute of it and Hope practicing "observing." But the pass was still, too still, and Fargo felt the uneasiness push at him. His eyes narrowed, he swept the surrounding hills again with a slow glance. Nothing stirred and he grimaced. A sudden burst of motion to the right showed a half-dozen deer leaping in their seemingly effortless, bounding springs, which meant they had been startled. Automatically, Fargo's hand went to the butt of the Colt at his hip. This was still Blackfoot country, but they were nearing the top edge of it, and Fargo shifted uneasily in the saddle. If the Blackfoot were going to strike, they'd have to do it soon. They wouldn't follow up past their territory. This wasn't the season for ambitious raids. This was the time for quick strikes near home, where preparations for the bone-chilling winter months had to go on.

Fargo's glance went to the sky and saw the sun had slipped into the afternoon. The hardness still in his eyes, he steered the pinto to where a half-dozen tall slabs of granite formed one side of the pass where it grew wide. "We'll wait here for the others," he said, and Hope's quick look showed she had caught the edge in his voice. Ted and Tim slid from their ponies and began to study the ground that led upward along the pass, their young faces full of grown-up seriousness.

Fargo saw Hope watching him. He stayed on the Ovaro, so she remained in the saddle. "Something's wrong," she murmured.

"Maybe not. Just playing safe," he said, and he gathered the ponies together and handed her both reins. "I want them in one place if you have to leave in a hurry," he said.

"Just playing safe," she echoed bitingly.

"That's right," he said, and her face told him she didn't believe him. He shrugged. He moved the pinto forward as Ted and Tim strayed farther up the pass, watching the boys with narrowed eyes. "That's far enough. Come on back here," he called, and both youngsters started back and busied themselves exploring the brush closer by. It was over an hour before the first wagon reached them and Fargo called the boys onto their ponies.

"Keep moving." Fargo waved to Abel Gunnard. He turned the pinto and rode on, but only a few yards in front of the wagons. When he found an arbor of stone and oak, he pulled the wagons inside and dismounted. "We'll camp here," he said, and watched the riders pull their mounts to one side to make room for the wagons.

Abel Gunnard stepped down from his big rack-bed,

Harriet following. Fargo felt the frown press into his brow as his eyes returned to Gabe Hazzard and his crew. The fact had registered only in a dim, offhand way, but it had stayed with him nonetheless and now he swept over the men with a quick glance. Two were missing, he saw, and he caught Gabe Hazzard watching him.

"Akins and Simpson," Fargo bit out. "Where are they?"

"They saw pheasant in the hills and went off to bring a pheasant dinner back," the foreman said.

"When?" Fargo snapped.

"About fifteen minutes ago, just before we reached you," Hazzard said.

"I said nobody rides out without my say-so," Fargo snapped.

"I couldn't stop them. They were still pretty sore about last night. Most of the men are," Hazzard said.

"And you're not going to treat them like kids," Fargo finished for him.

Gabe Hazzard's shrug was half-obstinacy, half-apology.

"You're overdoing this, Fargo," Abel Gunnard cut in. "Keep your rules for the boys and the womenfolk."

Fargo turned on Abel, his eyes frozen like ice. "How long do you figure it'll take them to bag their birds and get back?" he rasped.

"Half-hour, hour at the most," Gunnard said.

Fargo nodded, strode to a slab of rock, and sat down on it, his chiseled handsomeness as if carved of stone.

The others began to make camp: Eb Story gathered enough wood for a fire and Vera called the boys into her wagon.

Hope came over to him and sat down. "You just going to sit there and wait?" she asked.

"An hour can go damn fast," he said. "I watch these good folks wrestle with a lot of second thoughts," he said. He turned with surprise as Hope leaned her head back against the stone.

"Two can wait as easily as one," she said.

"Is that a vote of confidence?" he asked.

"No, curiosity," she returned, and he lapsed into silence.

The hour passed even more quickly than he anticipated, and he waited another fifteen minutes before getting to his feet, his gaze fastened on Abel Gunnard and Hazzard where they were clustered with the rest of the men.

"You want to wait another hour?" he asked harshly.

Gabe Hazzard's grim face stared back. "We'll go looking now," he said.

"No, you'll stay right here with the wagons. Post sentries. I'll go look for them," Fargo said.

"I want to go along," Hope said at his elbow.

He started to snap refusal at her but hesitated and held the reply on the tip of his tongue. She'd been pressing to absorb, learn, position herself for going on. He'd let her learn a lesson she'd never forget.

"Stay close and stay quiet," he said, and swung onto the Ovaro.

She took her horse and rode half a pace behind him as he went down the pass the way the wagons had come. He found the tracks where the two men had left the pass and gone into the thick tree cover on the right side. They'd gone almost straight, pushed through heavy brush, and left a trail of bruised leaves and snapped young twigs.

Fargo held the Ovaro at a slow walk, his every sense alert, one hand on the butt of the Colt. The brush was too heavy for pheasant. They needed clearer space to take wing, and Fargo followed the trail until he saw the trees suddenly thin out. He heard the horse first, blowing air and moving aimlessly, and then he spotted the animal. He moved forward carefully, halted again, and drew in deep breaths of air. They had been here, he muttered silently, the scent of bear grease and fish oil still in the air. But he smelled something else, the unmistakable odor of blood still fresh yet beginning to cake, the scent that a wolf could pick up a hundred yards away.

He steered the pinto left and cast a glance at Hope. She was almost at his side, apprehension in her face as she picked up his tenseness. He guided the pinto around a pair of Engelmann spruce that blocked his view directly ahead, and pulled to a sharp halt. The man's body lay against the base of an elm, stripped naked. Fargo peered past the streaks of blood that ran down the man's face and saw it was Akins, and he heard Hope's sharp gasp, a sound of shock and horror. Various parts of Akins had been cut off, from scalp to crotch, including both little fingers.

Hope's face was chalk-white and she stared, transfixed, until, with a cry of horror, she pulled her eyes away. "My God. Oh, my God," she whispered.

"The Blackfoot are big on souvenirs," Fargo said.

"I'm going to be sick," Hope murmured, and Fargo's arm shot out, his hand closing around the neck of her shirt, and he yanked her head up.

"No, you're not," he barked harshly. "You're not going to let it spill out of you and be cleaned. You're going to let it curl in your stomach so you can't forget it." He took his hand from her shirt, grabbed the reins of her horse, and turned the animal with the Ovaro as he began to move away. Hope rode with her head up, lips tight, and he saw her swallow hard a half-dozen times. They reached the pass with dusk settling in, and her lips finally moved, her voice a strained whisper.

"Will they be attacking us now?" she asked.

"No," he said. "I caught sight of them earlier. No war party, a few braves out to maybe bring in some more deer pelts. And pick up a scalp if they could."

She said nothing more and they reached the place where the wagons were pulled into a half-circle.

Fargo dismounted, watched Hope slowly get off the gelding as the others gathered, waiting in their faces. "You tell them," he said coldly.

She gathered anger in her eyes as she looked at him. "Bastard," she hissed, but she turned back to the others and, holding her voice steady, told of finding Akins. She left nothing out and he gave her credit for that. When she finished she turned and walked stiffly to the Conestoga and Fargo saw Vera follow her inside the wagon.

"I didn't look to find Simpson. Seemed no point to it," Fargo said, and watched the others exchange sober glances.

"Shouldn't we go give them a proper burial?" Gunnard said.

"I want six men here with the wagons. That leaves four, three if you take out Eb. Any volunteers?" Fargo asked, and only silence answered. Slowly, the men turned away, their heads bowed, and Fargo tethered the Ovaro and sat down against a tree.

Eb Story served another meal of beans and pork and everyone ate in silence except for Ted and Tim, but even they were subdued. In surprise, he saw Hope emerge from the Conestoga just as the meal ended.

"Got some left over," Eb said to her, but she shook her head and passed him.

Fargo waited as she strode up.

"Vera still wants to go on," she said. "We all know there's danger and savagery here. Maybe more than I expected," she conceded. "But we have to go on. We have to find out what happened to Tom. I'm sure Abel will still want to go on."

"I'm sure," Fargo said laconically.

"But it's plain that we need you more than ever now," she said. "Go on with us, please."

He frowned up at her. "I don't believe what I'm hearing," he said.

"Maybe because you can't understand," she answered.

"I'll do this for you. I'll take the boys back with me," he said, and saw the surprise flood her face.

"Why would you do that?" she asked.

"Because they're the innocent. They deserve more than being made part of Abel Gunnard's crazy dreams, their ma's obsession, and your stupid loyalty. They deserve to grow up. I'll find a place for them," he said.

"Vera'd never go along with that, putting them with strangers, people she doesn't even know," Hope said.

"She'd rather risk their being dead on a mountain. Great thinking," Fargo snapped.

"Dammit, all you can see is failure," Hope erupted angrily. "Well, the rest of us don't look only on the black side of things. We have hope, faith, determination. Everybody that goes west knows there's danger and death, but a lot of them overcome."

"They're not going through Blood Pass," Fargo said.

The anger stayed in her eyes. "You know what I think?" she flung at him. "I think you're plain afraid, that's what."

He smiled. She wanted to strike back, hurt, goad him into reversing himself. "Afraid's better than stupid," he said softly.

"Go to hell," she snapped, and strode away.

He took his bedroll, walked to the far side of the campsite, and welcomed sleep. He was weary, but the weariness was more inner than outer.

4

The morning came in with the sun fighting through long streaks of grayish clouds; the air changed from crisp to cold. Fargo rose, put away his bedroll and donned a jacket as he took a cup of coffee from Eb Story. Harriet came out with Abel, a wool sweater over her ample breasts, her usual half-pout replaced with a grim seriousness. The excess lipstick was also gone, and she looked both older and softer. Gabe Hazzard's crew came around, the men still subdued, and Vera emerged from her wagon to accept a cup of coffee with a nod. Only the boys were small whirlwinds of energy as they engaged in a game of tag around the wagons.

Fargo felt uneasy, and he knit his brow. One person was missing. "Where's Hope?" he asked.

"She rode off first thing this morning. I was just getting a fire started for coffee," Eb Story said.

"Rode off where?" Fargo asked.

"Up the pass," Story said.

"And you let her?" Fargo barked.

"Hell, I couldn't stop her. I told her you'd be mad, but she said she knew what she was doing, said she'd be waiting for us on a ways," the man answered.

"Goddamn," Fargo said. "Damn-fool girl."

"You know where she's gone? And why?" Gunnard asked.

"Yes, dammit," Fargo said, and threw the saddle on the Ovaro.

"You say something to her last night to make her do this?" Harriet asked accusingly.

"Nothing I haven't said before. She's been building up to this, to proving it inside herself. Damn fool," Fargo bit out as he sent the Ovaro racing past the others and onto the dry ground of Blood Pass.

He spotted the hoofprints of Hope's gelding at once and kept the Ovaro at a gallop. She had perhaps an hour's head start, an hour into the new day when the Blackfoot hunting parties would be on the prowl. His lips pulled back in distaste as he raced forward, finally slowing the Ovaro to give himself the chance to scan the morning high land where the mists still clung in opaque pockets. The hoofprints on the dry soil of the pass showed that Hope had slowed her horse as the pass grew steeper, and Fargo saw the high land on both sides become a series of rolling hills.

Something flashed ahead and to his right, just where the pass went into a curve. The flash came again and he saw the four near-naked horsemen, the sun flashing off a silver ornament at the front of a headband. He lost sight of the four Indians as he went into the curve. When he came out at the other end, he spied Hope ahead of him, riding at a trot along the pass.

He glimpsed the four figures to the right again, saw them moving down the hill toward Hope. He flicked a glance to the left of the pass, almost certain of what he'd see. The oath hissed from his lips. Three more Blackfoot snaked down toward Hope, and Fargo saw she was completely unaware of their presence. He spurred the Ovaro forward.

Hope heard the sudden sound of hoofbeats pounding into the soil, turned in surprise, and pulled to a halt. "I rather expected you'd be along," she said coolly.

"I'm not the only company you've got, honey," Fargo snapped, and her eyes went past him to where the four braves at the right had come into open view. Surprise flooded her face, but was quickly replaced by fear when she saw the other three riders appear. Her nervous eyes jerked to Fargo.

"What do we do?" she asked.

"I'm going to run like hell," Fargo said. "I'd suggest you do the same."

"We'll stay together," she said.

"That gelding of yours is never going to keep up with my Ovaro," Fargo said. "Sorry."

"You bastard," she exploded.

"No sense in both of us getting killed," Fargo shot back. "You wanted to play trailsman. Go ahead, honey." He spun the Ovaro and raced off into the hills where the three braves had just come down to the pass.

"Bastard," he heard Hope call. A quick glance back caught her spurring the gelding forward into a gallop. She stayed on the relatively smooth ground of the pass. Her best move, he approved silently. The gelding could outrun the Indian ponies on a straight line. But he'd tire quickly and they wouldn't, Fargo projected, and turned his attention to the three braves, who swerved in unison to go after him while the other four pursued Hope. Fargo turned the Ovaro up a green patch of hillside and plunged into heavy woods, where he had to slow at once. He saw the three braves shorten the distance to the trees by cutting at an angle across the low hill, and he moved deeper into the thick woodland before he halted, slid from the saddle, and drew the Colt when he spied the three riders in the trees.

The Blackfoot had grown cautious at once; they slowed and began to spread out. His gaze narrowed on the nearest of the three. One shot only, he reminded himself. The other four were probably still within earshot, and a single shot would carry proof that he was still alive, still being pursued. He took aim, paused to make sure where the other two were. One had gone to the left and moved carefully forward, the other a shadowy figure moving through the thick foliage far to the left.

He returned his gaze to the brave that came almost straight toward him. The Indian would spot the Ovaro in a moment, he realized, and Fargo's finger tightened on the trigger of the Colt. He aimed slightly low, allowing for the kick of the gun. The shot split the stillness of the thick woods.

The Blackfoot's chest erupted in a shower of bone and blood, yet the Indian somehow managed to emit a hoarse cry as he went back over the rump of his pony. His cry was echoed by two others, angry, bloodthirsty screams, and he saw the other two braves whirl and start toward him, following the sound of the shot. He slapped the Ovaro on the rump and the horse skittered forward through the forest in surprise. On one knee, Fargo saw both Blackfoot swerve their ponies to go after the horse. He dropped the Colt on the ground and moved quickly to yank the thin, double-edged throwing knife from the sheath around his calf. He chose the Indian nearest him as the brave swung his horse after the Ovaro. The knife whistled through the air. Fargo saw the blade hurtle into the Blackfoot's back, right between the shoulder blades. The Indian stiffened, flung both arms out sideways, and his head arched back for an instant. His arms were still flung stiffly out as he toppled to the ground. Fargo ran toward the prone form at once, only to skid to a halt as he saw the third Indian charging toward him on his pony.

He had heard the second brave fall or spotted the riderless Ovaro and turned back at once, Fargo realized as he saw the heavy stone tomahawk in the man's hand. The Blackfoot swerved his horse and the animal answered with a quick, nimble-footed response as the Indian threw the tomahawk. Fargo managed to fling himself sideways just in time; he felt the edge of the weapon graze his shoulder. He started to pull the Colt out and stopped. The others might still be close enough to hear another shot, which would bring at least two more racing back. He wanted the silence that would let them think he'd been caught and slain, so he stayed in a crouch as the brave leapt from his pony with easy grace.

The tomahawk lay at the base of an oak only a few

feet away from him. Fargo started to race for it, then cast a glance at the Indian and saw the Blackfoot yank a trapper's steel-bladed hunting knife from the belt of his breechclout. Unable to stop his forward motion, Fargo twisted and flung himself sideways as the Blackfoot lunged forward and brought the blade down in a vicious chopping motion. Fargo felt it tear through the edge of his jacket sleeve and go into the ground, and he rolled, kicked out with one leg, and caught the Blackfoot in the calf as the Indian pulled his knife free. The brave went down on one knee for a moment, but it was enough for Fargo to regain his feet and face his attacker. The Blackfoot rose, a lithe, smallish figure with only his black eyes showing any expression. He began to circle, the hunting knife held ready to slash out in any direction. Fargo backed as he circled and drew the Colt. The Blackfoot halted, eyed the gun. Fargo motioned to the knife, gestured to the ground. "Drop it," he said. He gestured again and knew the Blackfoot understood.

But the Indian moved toward him again, realizing Fargo didn't want to fire the gun or he'd have done so already. Fargo swore silently and circled left. He feinted, made a quick move to the other side, and the red man slashed out with the knife, a flat lunge that missed its target by inches. But Fargo had expected the Indian's reaction and brought the barrel of the Colt down in a short arc. It smashed into the brave's wrist and he dropped the knife with a grunt of pain. As he tried to follow the knife to the ground, Fargo brought his knee up and smashed it into the Indian's jaw. The man collapsed, fell on his side, and tried to roll over. Fargo brought the gun barrel down with all his strength, and the Blackfoot's forehead split open from top to bottom. He twitched and lay still, his face quickly drenched in red. Fargo stepped back, holstered the Colt, and hurried to where the Ovaro had halted in the trees.

He climbed onto the horse and hurried out of the woodland, down the hill to the pass, and followed the hoofprints of the Indian ponies. The pass rose upward, leveled off, and rose again. He slowed when the hoofprints halted and saw where the horses had circled, come together again, and stomped hard into the ground. They had caught up to Hope here, Fargo swore grimly and peered ahead to where the unshod hoofprints fell into line again. But this time a pair of footsteps mixed in with the hoofprints, and Fargo saw they had left the pass at a spot where a granite wall opened up onto another side passage. The passage made a wide circle through stone and tree-covered mountain land and began to turn back downward through a gulley. He rode over a low rise in the passage and saw the four Blackfoot some fifty yards ahead. They rode in pairs and dragged Hope behind them on foot, a rawhide strap around her neck. One of the Indians held her horse beside his pony. Fargo halted the pinto, slid to the ground, and drew the big Sharps from its saddle holster.

The Blackfoot rode their ponies at a walk, perhaps expecting their companions to join them somewhere. Fargo saw Hope stumble, fall, and cry out as she was dragged along until she managed to regain her feet and half-run, half-stumble on. He moved to the side of the gulley and clambered onto a low rise covered with serviceberry scrub trees. Settling into a long, loping stride, Fargo moved forward and quickly caught up to the four braves, slowing when he was opposite and slightly above them. He had a closer look at the round medallion in the headband that had caught the morning sun's rays. Made of hammered silver, it was an ideal target, he took note, the brave wearing it riding a few paces in front of the others. He carried a rifle, the others armed with bows they carried slung over one shoulder.

The one with the rifle would be the most dangerous, Fargo knew, but the one holding the rawhide rope around Hope's neck would have to be his first target. The Indian could snap her neck with one yank, and he'd do so the minute the shooting started.

Fargo moved on a few yards farther, dropped to one

knee, and raised the Sharps to his shoulder. He drew a bead on the Blackfoot holding Hope, fixed the position of the one with the medallioned headband in his mind, and fired. The Indian flew from his mount as though yanked by unseen wires and the others turned, startled. But Fargo had already swung the rifle and had the round, silver medallion centered in his sights. He fired and saw the bullet strike exactly in the center of the medallion, tear a hole through it, and enter the man's forehead. The Indian's head seemed to almost fly from his neck.

Hope had dropped to the ground and was trying to crawl toward the brush, but one of the two remaining Blackfoot had spun and started toward her. Fargo drew the Colt and fired two shots. Both hit the Indian just as he reached Hope, and his last steps were jerking, spasmodic motions before he fell. Hope rolled and managed to avoid his body as he hit the ground, but Fargo's eyes were on the fourth brave. The Indian had reached his pony, flung himself onto its back, and hung almost off the far side as the horse raced away.

Fargo lowered the Colt, the target impossible to hit even for him. The brave would race back to the main camp, somewhere deeper in the lower range, and the Blackfoot chiefs would do nothing. This was a time for more important things than pursuing a few stupid whites bent on suicide. They'd let the Nez Percé finish the job.

Fargo picked up the Sharps and moved down the side of the rise as Hope pushed to her feet, dusted herself off, and pulled the rawhide rope from her neck. Her round eyes held relief and apology and an edge of truculence.

"Thank you for coming back," she said. "I thought—"

"I know what you thought," he interrupted coldly. "If I'd stayed, they'd have gotten both of us."

"Leading three away gave you a chance at them," she said.

"Go to the head of the class," he muttered. "And if this was a regular schoolhouse, I'd suspend you for the term."

The truculence deepened in her face. "It wasn't all my doing. It was as much your fault," she glowered.

"My fault?" he almost shouted. "My fault?"

"You keep saying you're not going to stay. Somebody's going to have to break trail," she said.

"Of course. That's what all the riding along and asking questions was about. I just didn't think you'd be damn fool enough to think you could do it," Fargo pushed back at her. "Hell, breaking trail isn't just looking and listening. It's learning to read the earth and the trees, the wind and the sky. It's paying attention to everything that walks, runs, or crawls. It's learning not just what things are but what they mean. Damn, you think you can pick that up in a few excursions?"

"I had to do it," she said firmly.

"No, that was just plain orneriness. You didn't have to do it," he shot back.

"Are you saying you'll stay and take us through?" she countered with quick craftiness, her brown eyes snapping.

"No, I'm not saying that," he answered.

"Then I'll have to do it," she said.

He blew his breath out in exasperation. She was fighting, in her own ways, trying to reach him, playing on his sympathy, honor, whatever she could seize hold of. It would be easy to let her win, except that it would be signing her death warrant, signing it for all of them. He'd yet to make them understand that. "Get your stubborn ass on your horse," he said harshly. "We can talk some more later."

He swung onto the Ovaro and started off, and she caught up to him and rode in silence beside him. She didn't speak until they were in sight of the wagons. "Thank you, again," she said, her voice small. "You could have left me. Fools deserve leaving."

"Or saving," he muttered. As she rode on to the wagons, he saw the little smile, a hint of smugness in it, and swore silently. He turned his horse, waved Gunnard on to follow, and started back along the dry dirt of Blood Pass. Somehow, he'd have to keep trying to make them see before it was too late. But he would not go farther than that, Hope Maxwell's smug cleverness notwithstanding. He put away further musing and concentrated on the land that rose up ahead of him.

They had come onto the middle range now and the trees were changing more than colors. Like a changing of the guard, the hackberry, oak, elm, and ironwood were giving way to the great spruce and juniper, the lodgepole pine, and the white fir and balsam. Blood Pass continued to move up through mountain land that branched off into craggy spires and sometimes a sudden mountain draw or gulley. He saw it grow steeper and halted, scanned the land with his eyes narrowed. A small, winding passage broke off from the main pass and he sent the Ovaro along its curving route. It rose less sharply, curved perhaps two miles before winding its way back to the main trail. He returned along the curved passage and met the wagons just as they reached the place where the pass grew steep.

"We'll take that curved passage," he said.

Abel Gunnard stood up on the driver's seat of his wagon and peered on along the passage. "That's going out of the way." He frowned.

"I know that. I just rode it," Fargo said with a trace of impatience.

"I'd guess it'll take us at least four hours longer," Gunnard said. "Maybe till the end of the day."

"Probably," Fargo said. "But the main road is too steep for the heavy load you have in that supply wagon."

Abel Gunnard looked up at the main part of the pass. "I say they can make that," he replied, and Fargo saw Gabe Hazzard nod in agreement.

"I'd say so, too," Fargo remarked, and Gunnard frowned at him. "But it'll take a hell of a lot out of your horses," he added. "They won't be fit for hard pulling for two, maybe three days."

"You keep saying time's important," Gunnard said.

"It is. So's keeping your team fit," Fargo said.

With a hardly audible mutter, Abel Gunnard turned

his wagon and followed Fargo down the curving passage. Fargo let the others turn into the passage before riding on, but he hurried the horse while his eyes scanned the higher land on both sides. When he spied another narrow passage that branched off, wide enough for only one horse, he spurred the pinto up it and halted on a narrow ledge that let him see the entire terrain. Gunnard and the others were still back on the first part of the curving passage, moving carefully. He squinted back down Blood Pass. Rock sides and trees combined to cover much of it, but he saw nothing that moved along the trail, so he retraced his steps to the passage and rode on to join the main trail of the pass.

Daylight had started to fade when the wagons finally arrived. He led the way to a spot where the pass leveled off and provided a place to halt for the night. "Don't expect much traffic going through," he said laconically. As night fell and Eb Story dished up supper, he saw Hope regard him with faint amusement in her round eyes.

"Find anything when you rode that little side passage?" she asked, and smiled smugly at the surprise in his gaze. "I saw the hoofprints as we passed, a single rider," she added.

"Still playing trailsman?" he muttered.

"Just keeping in practice," she said tartly.

"You do that," he said, turning away as Ted and Tim ran up to him. "Ma said it was all right with her if we rode some with you tomorrow," Tim said.

Fargo considered it for a moment. "Guess tomorrow would be all right," he said. "We'll be in middle range, beyond Blackfoot land and not yet in Nez Percé country."

"Then we can go?" Tim asked excitedly.

"Just us," Fargo said with a glance at Hope.

She bristled at once. "That's not fair. You won't agree to stay and you won't let me learn as much as I can."

"Because you can't learn enough. You'll only get yourself killed," he threw back.

"We won't quit, no matter what you try," she snapped, and strode away.

"Only thing I'm trying to do is help you, dammit," he called after her, but she continued to march away.

Tim's voice cut into the moment. "We heard Hope tell Ma you saved her life. Why's she so mad at you, then?" the boy asked out of innocent confusion.

"Some things are so foolish you have to be grown up to understand them," Fargo said, his hand resting on the boy's head. "I just hope you get the chance," he added grimly. "See you in the morning."

Both boys gave him a quick embrace and ran back to their Conestoga.

Fargo got his bedroll from the pinto and set his gear off the main pass in a small creviced space between shrubs and a boulder. The cold of the mountains had seized the night and he undressed quickly. He had just slid into the warmth of his bedroll when he saw the figure moving across the pass between wagons. The moon outlined the shoulder-length hair and Fargo sat up as the figure came toward him. She halted at the end of the bedroll, her eyes on him. She wore a black cape she held tight to her.

"This is a surprise," he said.

"Don't get the wrong idea," Hope said firmly. "I just have some things I want to say."

"I'm tired. Make them short," Fargo muttered.

"Regardless of everything else, I am very grateful for what you did today," she said. "I can't do more than say thank you."

"Want some suggestions?" Fargo inquired.

"Dammit, can't you accept a simple thank-you?" she flared.

"Can't you stop being fools, you and all the others?" he tossed back.

"You're impossible," she said, spun on her heel, and stalked away. He watched her disappear into the darkness beside the wagons, then he lay back and closed his eyes. The cold night wind swept over him, a kind of grim lullaby that put him to sleep quickly.

Morning came in clear and cold with a good sun. The boys were waiting on their ponies before he finished his coffee. He led them up the pass, moving at an easy pace as he saw the others only half-ready to roll.

"What kind of Indians are you looking for now, Fargo?" Ted asked.

"None yet. But in another few days I'll be looking for the Nez Percé," Fargo answered.

"Where'd they ever get a name like that?" Tim asked.

"The early French explorers gave them that name. It means 'those with the pierced noses.' The Nez Percé often hang gold rings, shells, or beads through their noses," Fargo explained to his wide-eyed listeners, who followed with a flurry of questions as they rode beside him. In between answers he managed to scan the land: the evergreens grew more plentiful, the oaks and hackberry remaining almost bare of leaves now. His eyes shifted from distant peaks to the sky and back to the trail at his feet. When he dismounted and stooped down to the ground, Ted and Tim were at his side instantly.

He lifted a handful of dirt in his hand and let it trickle back through his fingers.

"What is it?" Tim questioned.

"Dry, too damn dry," Fargo said. "It's been a long time since there's been any rain."

"That'll keep the ground easy for the wagons, won't it?" Ted asked.

"Here and now," Fargo said. "But I'm worrying about a place we'll be reaching in a few days."

"A dangerous place?" Tim questioned.

"Yes, the drier, the more dangerous," Fargo said.

"What do we do when we reach it?" Ted questioned.

"There's a way past. It's real hard, but it can take us past," Fargo answered, and laughed at the excitement shining in their eyes. It was all glorious adventure; danger and death were mere words to them. But they weren't just words, he grimaced. They were real, lurking in wait, ready to strike at the first chance. He shook his head as the sourness surged through him. He sent the boys hunting blackberries in a patch he spotted off the road. While they picked the berries, he swept the distant path of the pass back the way they had come, spotted the wagons for a brief moment, and lost them again behind the high rocks. But his gaze had stayed down at the far end of the pass where the oak and hackberry still bordered the main trail on both sides. Finally, when he turned away and leaned back against a blue spruce, his eyes were narrowed in thought.

When the boys finished, returning with a sack of blackberries, he spotted two wild turkeys, took the Sharps, and followed the birds through a spruce forest until he brought both down. He let the boys drag them back to the main pass with glee and waited for the first wagon to arrive. He gave Eb Story the birds so he could start preparing them.

Ted and Tim, showing signs of weariness, elected to stretch out in the Conestoga for the rest of the day. Fargo went on, ignoring the glare Hope tossed his way, and finally watched the sun slip down below the high peaks. He picked out a place to camp, this time off the pass in a spruce-bordered alcove. When the others arrived and the cook began to roast the turkeys on makeshift spits, Fargo took his bedroll to a small circle of raised ground that let him see the pass and the camp beside it.

"Expecting trouble?" Gabe Hazzard asked when Fargo returned to sit down for the meal.

"Not really," Fargo answered. "But we're being followed." The foreman frowned in surprise. "I saw movement way back down the pass when I was riding with the boys," Fargo said.

"Ma Cowley, probably?" Gabe Hazzard said.

"No wagon," Fargo said. "One rider at most, staying in tree cover but hurrying."

"Nez Percé already?" the foreman offered.

"Doubt it. Anyway, they'd likely be coming down

from above us, not following behind," Fargo said. "Maybe a trapper or a prospector going his own way, really."

"Likely," Gabe Hazzard said, finished his meal, and went off with his men.

The fire burned itself down and Fargo rested a while longer beside the wagons. Hope was hanging two blouses from the tail of her Conestoga. She saw him when he rose to his feet, and drew a blue robe tighter around her neck.

"I'm going out with you, come morning," she said firmly.

"What if I say no?" he asked mildly.

"I'm not going off by myself. You've no reason to refuse me," she said.

"I've a dozen I can think of without trying," he said. "I'll sleep on it."

She glared at him. As she stepped into the wagon, the robe fell open to reveal a lovely, long, lithe leg. He turned away as she disappeared inside the wagon, and went to his saddlebag, where he rummaged around at the bottom and finally drew out a spool of darning thread.

The camp pretty much asleep, Gabe Hazzard's crew at the other end of the alcove, he silently made his way a half-dozen yards down the main trail of the pass. Kneeling, he tied one end of a length of the darning thread around the bottom of a young sapling and brought the other end across the pass so that it strung about two feet above the ground, invisible in the blackness. He gave the thread a single turn around a thin branch on the other side of the road and stretched the rest of it to his bedroll.

He ran the thread over a low branch and took out his Colt, tied the end of the thread around the trigger guard, and stepped back. The revolver hung at the end of the thread and swayed gently in the night breeze. If the thread across the road were broken, the gun would fall to the ground with more than enough of a thud to wake him. He slid into his bedroll only six inches away from the hanging revolver and closed his eyes. He had stretched the thread high enough to avoid being snapped by raccoons, skunks, or other small critters. Now all he had to do was get some sleep. The rest, if it was to happen, would do so on its own. He turned and let sleep embrace him.

The night moved on and a half-moon slid across an early-winter sky. Below, the ground hardened as if in silent answer to a soundless song. Fargo slept as he always slept, as the denizens of the wild slept, a sub-conscious part always alert, ever ready to respond to the slightest sudden sound. When the dull thud came, he snapped awake instantly, his body jackknifing upward, his hand reaching out to pick up the Colt. He blinked, cleared his eyes, and peered through the night and saw the horse and rider moving slowly up the pass toward the campsite. Flinging himself from the bedroll, he moved downward on silent steps, slid down the short wall of shrubs toward the pass below, and reached it just as the horse arrived at the same spot. The frown creased his brow at once as he saw the blond hair, almost silvery in the light of the half-moon.

"I'll be dammed," he breathed aloud, and raised the Colt as Cassie halted the horse and peered at the sleeping camp. "Don't move," Fargo said in a voice only she could hear.

Her face turned toward the sound of his voice. "I'm alone," she said softly.

Fargo peered down the pass as far as the night would let him see—waited, watched—but no other riders appeared.

"It's just me, honest," Cassie said. "I ran away."

Fargo walked toward her and holstered the Colt. She wore a wool three-quarter-length jacket over the single-piece dress and still managed to look appealing in a waiflike way. "You been trying to catch up all day?" he asked.

"Yes." She nodded. "But I had to stay in the trees. I was afraid they'd be coming after me."

"Zeb and Zane?" Fargo asked.

Cassie nodded again and slid from the horse. "I've been trying to get away for so long. I finally got the chance and took it," she said.

"Where are they?" Fargo asked.

"Back, at least a whole day, maybe more. Ma Cowley took you at your word," Cassie said. She came toward him, but halted close to him, her light-blue eyes full of pleading. "Let me stay with you," she said. "I can't go back. I never wanted to stay, but they made me. I'll help, do whatever anyone wants me to do. Just let me stay. Please don't send me back to Ma Cowley." She blinked to fight back tears, looking as helpless and vulnerable as a six-year-old.

"All right, for tonight, at least. We'll talk more, come morning," Fargo said, and her arms flew around his neck. Her feet left the ground as she clung to him.

"Thank you," she whispered. "I kept telling myself you wouldn't turn me away."

"This way," he said, and led her around the back to where he had bedded down above the pass. "No sense in waking the whole camp up tonight." She tied her horse to a low branch, took a blanket from her saddle-bag, shed the wool jacket, and lay down a half-dozen feet from his bedroll. She pulled the dress off and he saw the lovely, rounded shoulders before they disappeared under the blanket.

"Thank you, Fargo," Cassie murmured.

"No promises. It's Abel Gunnard's wagon train," Fargo said.

"We'll talk, come morning. I've got a lot to explain to you," Cassie said.

"You can say that again, honey," Fargo grunted, and watched her turn on her side. She was asleep in minutes, the even sound of her breathing drifting through the night to him. Her appearance had been a surprise, but no more so than the first time he'd seen her, he reminded himself and smiled as he returned to sleep.

When he opened his eyes with the morning sun, he saw Cassie dressed, beside her horse, folding her blanket. She'd used her canteen to wash and her face still glistened. Her eyes were bright as she threw a smile at him. She turned away as he rose, washed, and pulled on clothes. When he finished, she came toward him. Once again he saw how she was both seductive and waiflike, an unlikely but effective combination.

"You talk to the others. I'm not good with most people," she said. "But I feel different talking to you. I was sold to Ma Cowley when I was ten. My pa sold me to her. I never knew anything different, but I knew one day I had to get away. This is my chance, Fargo, maybe my one chance." She took a step closer and laid her palm against his chest. "I know it won't make much difference, but I'd like a chance to finish what we started that first morning," she said. "I've never wanted that with any of the others. Truth is, I never did it with any of them, never."

"Your joining up with this wagon train could be one more mistake. That second chance you want could be a very short one," he told her. "They'll never make it through Blood Pass."

Cassie frowned as she took in his words. "Why are you sticking with them?" she asked.

"I'm still hoping I can make them see facts," he said.

Cassie shrugged. "It's still my only chance. I'll stay if you do, and go if you go," she said with a combination of resignation and trust that was impossible to turn aside.

"Let's get some coffee," Fargo said, and she fell in beside him as he walked down to the campsite.

Gabe Hazzard was taking a tin cup of coffee from Eb Story when Fargo came up with Cassie close beside him. The man's eyes grew wide.

"Company. She arrived late last night," Fargo said. "I told you somebody was following us."

The foreman stared in amazement and took a deep sip of his coffee. Harriet walked up with Abel, and the man's eyes grew wide as he saw Cassie.

"You were with Ma Cowley," Abel murmured.

"I was, but I ran as soon as I got the chance," Cassie said.

Fargo flicked a glance at the others as they emerged from their wagons and came up to listen. Hope, in the forefront, frowned at Cassie with a touch of disdain.

"She wants to stay here with us," Fargo said.

"And what do you say, Fargo?" Hope cut in, sarcasm coating her tone. "You were the one who refused to have any of them along."

He fastened Hope with a cool stare and she stared back. "Everybody deserves a second chance at life," he said. "I've told her this one could be short."

"Well, if it's all right with you, it's fine with me," Abel Gunnard said. "She can sleep in the supply wagon. We've some extra mattresses in there."

"Thank you, thank you so much," Cassie said, and flung her arms around Abel Gunnard for a quick embrace. "I can help drive. Ma Cowley made me drive her wagon a lot." With a quick, grateful smile at Fargo, Cassie took her horse and tied him to the tailgate of the supply wagon while the others began to drift away to finish their coffee.

Fargo turned to the Ovaro and paused as he saw Hope's coolly amused smile fastened on him.

"Forgive and forget. Turn the other cheek," she said. "Why do I have trouble seeing you in that role?"

"I'm full of surprises," Fargo growled.

"I'd say full of expectations," she slid at him, and he threw an icy stare at her.

"You feeling guilty?" he speared, and the cool smile vanished.

"That's a rotten thing to say, or expect," she snapped.

"You want to dish it out you have to take it, honey," he said, and she stalked to her wagon on angry, hard steps, the brown hair swinging as if in echo of her breasts, which bounced with each step.

Fargo returned Ted's and Tim's wave as both boys sat on the driver's seat of their Conestoga, their mother taking the reins. Cassie was talking with Eb Story as the Trailsman sent the Ovaro onto the pass and rode away. He kept the horse at a fast trot and stopped only to dismount and run his fingers across the ground. Each time he did, he felt the grimness curl around him. It was past the noon hour when he halted again, but he stayed in the saddle this time.

He peered up at the three high crags of sandstone that rose up along one side of the pass, his eyes narrowed as he slowly scanned the tall formations. The pass itself leveled out where it ran alongside the bottom of the three tall mountain forms and grew attractively wider. On the other side, a line of tall northern spruce grew along a low ridge of granite. Just where the main road of the pass leveled out, a narrow road branched off, much the same as the other road had done a few days back.

But this road was barely wide enough to accommodate one wagon at a time, and the roadbed was full of loose rocks. But with care—a great deal of care—it was passable. Fargo let a deep sigh escape as he slid from the Ovaro, seated himself against a rock, and waited.

Over another hour had gone by, perhaps two, when the wagons caught up to him, Abel Gunnard's rackbed in the lead with Gabe and his crew riding alongside. Fargo saw Hope had gone into second place, with the supply wagon behind, and she steered to a halt alongside Gunnard when he stopped. Fargo rose to his feet and Abel's question spoke for the others. "Something wrong?" he asked.

"Not yet," Fargo said.

"Meaning what?" Gunnard frowned and Harriet came out from inside the wagon to sit beside him.

"The Nez Percé call this the place of the sliding hills," he said.

"Those formations?" Gunnard asked, and pointed to the three high rocklike hills. Fargo nodded and Gunnard frowned. "They look solid enough to me," he said.

"Harriet looks like a blonde," Fargo said. "Looks are deceiving."

"You trying to tell me all of that slides down?" Gunnard pressed skeptically.

"Not all of it," Fargo said. "Just enough to bury you." He pointed at the main trail of the pass where it leveled off. "I can ride across that. Good soft footing under my horse, too. But I'd better ride slow and alone."

"Why would those formations slide down?" Gabe Hazzard asked.

"Because they're only solid underneath. Sandstone is formed by the action of wind, water, and ice. It's mostly grains of quartz, and to make it firm it needs a cement such as silica, lime, or iron. Most places that's what happens. But here, for some reason, the wind action is so constant that it keeps the grains from cementing. That means the outside of those formations are barely holding together. Any number of things can cause them to slide, and when they do, they come down in a huge sandslide of fine grains that choke, suffocate, blind, and bury you with their mass and weight," Fargo explained. "The place of the sliding hills."

"There's no certainty they'll come down," Gunnard said.

"No certainty." Fargo nodded. "Just for damn sure." He pointed to the narrow, rocky passage that led off to the back side of the ridge of spruce. "You can make it through that passage if you go real slow," he said, and saw Gunnard frown at once.

"Hell, look at those rocks. We'd be sure to break a wheel," the man said.

"Not if you take it very carefully," Fargo said.

"We take it careful enough to make it on that passage, we'll lose another two days," Gunnard protested.

"Most likely," Fargo admitted, and turned as Hope's voice cut in.

"I think Fargo's being clever," she said. The cool amusement was in her face again. "He wants us to keep losing time until it becomes obvious the snows will stop us from going on. First there was that part of the pass that was too steep. Now there's this."

Fargo's eyes narrowed at her. "That round-cheeked pretty face hides a nasty turn of mind, doesn't it?" he said.

"Oh, come now, Fargo. You've said you'll do your best to make us see we can't go on," she said. "Admit it. You're convinced we can't make it. You're just trying to make sure we have to turn back."

Fargo saw Abel Gunnard studying him, his lips pursed. He glanced at Gabe Hazzard and the man gave a half-shrug. "I do believe that Hope's touched on it, Fargo," Gunnard said. "I know you think you're doing the right thing. I'm not even mad about it. I just want you to stop."

"You're not mad? No, it's hard to be mad when you're blind," Fargo said, and turned his lake-blue eyes on Hope. "And you're an expert in only one thing, honey: being wrong," he said.

He spurred the Ovaro along the wagons and halted at the last one. Vera looked at him with her drawn face expressionless. "I'll take the boys riding with me," he said. The woman's eyes met his hard stare and he saw the racing thoughts behind them. She nodded finally, and he knew she wasn't certain why. But something had pushed hard enough inside her, and that's all he cared about for the moment.

Ted and Tim leapt from the wagon and ran to untie their ponies at the tailgate.

"I'd like to ride along with you," Cassie's voice said from nearby.

"Suit yourself," he answered, and she moved alongside him as the boys came up.

"You going to ride off on your own? Just 'cause Hope called your hand?" Gunnard frowned.

"It's Fargo's way of sulking," Hope sniffed.

"It's his way of staying alive," Fargo growled.

"I'll expect you to own up and apologize when we get past this," Gunnard said.

Fargo made no reply and watched Abel Gunnard wave the wagons forward. Gabe Hazzard took his crew out to ride ahead and Fargo stayed until the last

Conestoga, with Vera at the reins, rolled on. He turned the Ovaro into the rock-strewn narrow passageway and let the horse pick his own way until a small crevice of a trail appeared that led up to the low ridge of spruce. He beckoned to the others and took the Ovaro up the steep crevice, which quickly grew even narrower as the spruce crowded in on it. But it stayed passable, thanks to the deer that had eaten away the bark and low branches of the trees. When he reached the top he halted and waited for the others to catch up. The trees grew in a line along the top of the ridge and he could look down on the wagons that rolled along the level, smooth trail of the main pass, some fifty feet below.

"There's Ma," Ted said, and Fargo nodded, moving the pinto forward to keep almost abreast of the four wagons below, Gabe Hazzard and his crew riding just ahead of them.

"You really think something's going to happen?" Cassie asked.

"Christ, I hope I'm wrong," he said.

Cassie pointed to the wheel of Gunnard's wagon. "They're sinking down pretty deep," she said.

He nodded and saw Eb Story using the whip on the team pulling the supply wagon.

"You afraid they'll get stuck?" Cassie asked.

"No, the footing's firm enough underneath the surface sand," Fargo said. "But the more they have to pull, the more vibration they set up. And Gabe's got his boys riding too fast, dammit." Fargo's eyes went to the three towering formations, so deceptively solid to the eye. They seemed to frown down on the four wagons that edged their base, their silence almost stern and disapproving.

The riders had reached the center formation, started past it, and Fargo watched as Abel Gunnard rolled forward, Eb Story using the whip again on the team pulling the second big rack-bed.

Fargo moved forward, Cassie and the boys at his heels. He rode on to pull slightly ahead of the wagons, and his eyes scanned the towering formations again. Abel Gunnard's wagon had just passed the middle of the formations with only the last and tallest to pass. Fargo wiped his palms on his Levi's and realized he was perspiring.

Maybe old lore and Indian wisdom wouldn't hold up this time, he thought. He'd be happy for that, happy to give Abel Gunnard all the apology he wanted. He looked back down to the wagons again. Gunnard's lead rig had hit a soft spot and he took his whip, too. Fargo watched the horses pull the wagon forward, Gunnard and Eb Story still forcing their teams.

"Too fast, dammit. Too fast," he muttered, and his gaze went to the towering formations again. He had just returned his eyes to the wagons below when he heard the sound, a strange sound unlike any he had ever heard before, something in between a crackle and a hiss. He shifted his attention back to the rock formations. They were moving.

"Oh, my God," he hissed as the huge sandstone formations seemed to flow down all at once, millions and millions of fine particles of quartz sliding down to the pass. It was, he found himself thinking, not unlike a woman slithering into a filmy garment, and the strange crackling-hissing suddenly became a roaring sound.

The deluge of sliding grains became a huge wave when it reached the pass, surging forward, sweeping onto the four wagons. Fargo saw Gunnard's rig go over. Three of Gabe Hazzard's riders went down under the murderous wave.

"Ride!" Fargo barked. "Ride like hell!" He sent the Ovaro into a canter, swerved between the spruce, and reached the end of the ridge where it descended to join the main pass. When he came onto the pass, he swung the Ovaro around and started back. The terrible roaring sound had suddenly ended; the stillness was worse.

He reached the first mound of sand, took the horse over it until he began to bog down, and then leapt from the saddle. He looked back and saw the boys,

Cassie close behind, halt beside the Ovaro. "Come on, this way," he called. "You're light. You can make your way best." He turned back and fought his way over the mounds of grainy sand, saw an arm feebly waving, and reached it. He dug his feet into the shifting sand and yanked. Gabe Hazzard's head appeared. He pulled again and the man's shoulder came free and Gabe pushed himself from the loose sand.

"Pull out anybody you can find near the surface," Fargo said. "Get to the wagons." He peered ahead and saw part of Gunnard's wagon sticking above the grains. The surface rippled for a moment, then Gunnard's head slowly emerged. The man pulled himself free by hanging on to one of the wagon bows. He reached down and pulled Harriet into sight, sputtering and coughing and covered with sand. Ted and Tim had found one of Hazzard's men and were helping to pull him free. Fargo passed Gunnard on his way to Hope's Conestoga. The canvas top was still visible and he clawed his way through the mounds of sand. "Come on, dammit," he yelled at Gunnard. "The sand's still loose. There's a chance."

Gunnard shook away the shock on his face and floundered after Fargo. The supply wagon, heaviest and most unwieldy, hadn't turned over and now lay buried deep under rippling mounds of sand that Fargo pushed away to reach the Conestoga. He ripped the canvas still showing and used his hands to scoop away the loose grains. Hope's arm came into sight and he continued frantically pawing away the sand as Gunnard joined him. More of Hope appeared, her head and torso. He reached down, got an arm around her waist, and pulled her free. He flung her over his shoulder before putting her down on the canvas of the wagon. She was barely breathing. He pushed hard against her rib cage and she threw up a mouthful of sand. Her breathing grew stronger.

Gabe Hazzard came up and Fargo took a moment to bark orders at him. Gunnard, who still wore shock like a wreath around his neck, was too slow in moving.

"Get to Vera's wagon, dammit," Fargo yelled. Both men floundered away at once and Fargo half-lifted, half-slid Hope forward and hung her head down. She gave a gurgling sound, spit up again, and he felt her draw a clear breath as he pulled her to a sitting position. Her eyes opened, took a moment to focus on him, then stared with gathering shock and horror.

"Can you walk?" Fargo asked, and she nodded. "Go try to find some of the men," he said harshly, and trudged his way toward the last wagon, where Hazzard and Gunnard were scooping away sand. He saw Gabe reach down and lift Vera's limp form into view. They had exposed a corner of the Conestoga as they dug and Hazzard put her face down over it.

"God, she's breathing," Fargo heard the man say.

"Keep her head down. Push on her ribs. Keep her breath going," Fargo called out, and turned to look back over the mound of sandy grains. He saw that Ted and Tim, Cassie beside them, had dug out another of Gabe's men, and Hope had halted where a head and arm projected from the sand. She knelt down and began pulling. The man moved his head and then freed one arm. Fargo turned back to where Gunnard and Gabe Hazzard were holding Vera up between them and she was drawing in deep drafts of air.

Fargo slid down onto a mound of the sandy grains, his jaw a hard line as he looked up at the towering formations that remained staring down at them. "The place of the sliding hills," he muttered. The Nez Percé had named it well. He rose, finally, waiting while Gunnard and Gabe Hazzard reached him with Vera. Her eyes were open, fear and shock still in them, but she stared at Fargo as the two men held her between them. She took her eyes away for a moment and found the boys standing beside two of Gabe's men who sat on the sand. Her gaze drifted back to Fargo. "Thank you," she said. He nodded. There was no need for words, so he started away, lifting his legs in high steps through the soft and shifting sand.

He halted where Hope had stopped beside the boys

and the others who were alive. Gabe Hazzard made a quick count. "Only four of the boys left," the man said. "Damn."

"Any of the horses?" Fargo asked.

"I saw four of them manage to get away when it started," one of the men said.

"I saw Sam's horse throw him when the sand started going down. He hightailed it before Sam hit the ground. I think my horse might've made it too because he ran when I went over," another of the men said.

"The ones who made it will be stopped somewhere up the pass," Fargo said. "We can round them up later, or tomorrow. They won't go far."

"What do we do now?" Hope asked.

"I'll go find us a spot to bed down. The rest of you go to the wagons. Stay together, work together. Use your hands to dig out a few things for the night, then start walking up the pass. You'll find me," Fargo said. He turned, passed Hope without a glance at her, and trudged his way out of the billows of sandy grains. He motioned for Ted and Tim to follow him. Cassie had already begun to pull herself after him.

Once out of the mountain of sand, he waited for the boys to climb onto their ponies before mounting and leading the way. He found a place only a hundred yards on and rode into a clearing surrounded by spruce and balsam with a stepping-stone rock formation rising beyond the trees. He dismounted and had the boys start a fire as the cold stabbed through the late-afternoon sky. Dusk had begun to settle in when the others appeared, each carrying assorted bundles of gear and clothing. They sank down before the fire almost as one, and Abel Gunnard looked up at Fargo with exhaustion in his face. Harriet clung to his arm, her face blanched with shock. "I have a sack of turkey meat left over," Gunnard said, tossing a bag on the ground.

"We'll make do with it," Fargo said.

"I've some dried beef strips," Cassie said.

Fargo's eyes moved across the others with harshness. "There's only one reason any of you are alive," he said. "There was air in the sand when it came down. The grains were still loose, and when it swept over you, it didn't completely suffocate, though I'm sure it felt like it. Except for those it buried deep. Pure mass and weight were too much for them."

"What happens tomorrow?" one of the men asked. "I'm Abe Jones," he introduced.

"We got to the supply wagon, use our hands first, dig in enough to get to the shovels inside. Then we start shoveling a few million grains of quartz. I figure in two or three days we ought to have the wagons dug free enough to see if they're usable," Fargo said.

"And do some burying," Gabe Hazzard added solemnly.

"I brought blankets for the boys," Vera said. She rose, beckoned to Ted and Tim, and took them to the far side of the campsite.

Fargo gave Abel Gunnard a long, hard stare. "You said something about an apology earlier today," he murmured, and Abel Gunnard made a strangled sound, pushed himself to his feet, and rushed from the fire. He ran into the dark and the sounds of his retching drifted back to the dying fire.

"You didn't have to say that," Harriet said, a terrible sadness in her voice.

"I could've said more," Fargo snapped back harshly, and she made no reply. He rose, went to the Ovaro, and took his bedroll down while the fire burned out and the others prepared to settle down. None would sleep well, he was certain. He started across the campsite to climb up past the spruce when Hope's figure stepped from the shadows.

"No hard, hurting words for me?" she asked, and he saw she held herself very straight, hands clenched at her sides.

"You need any?" he asked coldly.

She stayed silent for another moment and suddenly he saw her lips quiver. She swallowed and tried to turn away, but the explosion of sobs was too fast. "Oh, God, oh, God," she managed to get out between the sobs that racked her body. "It was my fault, all my fault," she said.

"He was happy to go along with you," Fargo said, a small offering, he realized as she shook it away.

"My doing, mine," Hope gasped, shuddered, and half-turned to him. He offered no comforting arm and she stared back as the tears rolled down her round cheeks.

"You can't undo it," he said.

"Meaning what?" she asked.

"Meaning you'll have to live with it. Breaking yourself up won't change a damn thing, not for now, not for tomorrow," he said.

"That's cold comfort," she said.

"Better than none," he returned.

She nodded slowly and started to turn from him. She paused, then went on. He watched her disappear into the darkness, then moved on beyond the spruce, set down his bedroll, and felt the increasing cold of the night. It ought to be over, he knew, yet something told him it wasn't, and he grimaced as he turned on his side.

Little Cassie had behaved well and stayed in the background. Maybe she'd end up being the bright spot. Sleep came to him on that thought.

5

Morning came in cold with a weak sun, but three of
the horses had come back and some of the men went
out and found the other two. "Five—six, if we have to
use Cassie's," Fargo said. "Enough for three teams if
the wagons can roll. Let's find out. We'll start where
we left off, with the supply wagon."

He led the way back to the mounds of sand and
trudged to the partially exposed supply wagon. Their
hands became miniature shovels once again as they
began digging, tossing the sandy quartz aside as dogs
dig for bones. Part of what they threw aside promptly
slipped back again, but they kept at it, though the
others halted with increasing frequency to stretch ach-
ing arm and back muscles. It was hard and grim work,
yet Ted and Tim stayed right beside him.

Fargo stepped back from the sand when the wagon
began to take shape. "Rest a spell," he said. "Then
we keep on. We'll have her dug free in another hour."
He peered at the big wagon. It had been the most
heavily loaded and hadn't gone over. It seemed in
pretty good shape. When they resumed digging, they
were able to get at the shovels inside. With a shout of
triumph, Gabe Hazzard passed the shovels out to the
others and digging became almost pleasurable.

Even with the shovels, it took most of the day to
completely dig the wagon out. Fargo slowly walked
around it, his gaze taking in the undercarriage as he
bent low. "Nothing wrong anywhere," he said, and a
grateful murmur rippled through the others. "While
we have daylight left, let's shovel a path out of here,"

he said, and everyone began to throw aside sand again. It was Gabe Hazzard who suddenly stopped a dozen feet from the wagon, and Fargo knew what he'd found by the tightness in his face.

"Take the boys back to the camp," Fargo told Vera. Hope went with her while Gunnard, Hazzard, and the rest of the crew dug until Eb Story had been unearthed. They took him to the side, dug another sandy grave, and erected a marker over it. Abel Gunnard said the proper words.

Darkness had blanketed them by the time the sober moment was over. Fargo trudged back to the campsite with the others. There'd be no way or time to hunt for the rest of Gabe Hazzard's crew under the mountains of sandy grains. He sank down in the little clearing and felt the ache in his arms and back. Abe Jones had taken enough from the supply wagon to produce a simple but satisfying meal, which they ate in silence.

Hope sat with Vera, Harriet beside Gunnard, and the men clustered near Hazzard. Cassie sat near him and ate with gusto. For all her slender outer appearance, she seemed to be standing up right well, and she tossed him a quick smile whenever she caught his eyes on her. Hope had become almost an echo of her sister-in-law, silent and withdrawn. He rose and paused at her side as she cleaned off her plate before handing it to Abe Jones. Her glance at him was dark and full of anguish.

"I said live with it, not wallow in it," he remarked.

"You don't have it inside you," she said, and walked away with Vera. She wanted her guilt, he grunted silently. Maybe it'd be a mistake to soften it too soon. He shrugged as he took down his bedroll, and Cassie smiled shyly as she walked by and folded herself into her blanket. Finally he settled down for the night. The day's digging had been only a beginning, and he slept quickly, exhaustion an ally.

When morning came he ordered two teams brought through the pathway they'd cleared in the sand and hitched to the big rack-bed rig. He stood aside as

Gabe worked the horses until they pulled the heavy wagon through the still-clinging grains. The second team was unhitched when the wagon reached the clearing, and Fargo led the others back to the task of shoveling out Gunnard's lead wagon. He halted when they were halfway finished, the wagon on its side, the front wheels broken from the axle.

"Let's try Hope's Conestoga next," he said, and everyone began the task of shoveling again. The long, painfully slow process brought happier results this time as the Conestoga appeared to be intact, wheels and axles undamaged. By the time they had the wagon drawn out, the day was at an end and the exhausted figures returned to the camp. The digging had become more difficult and more unpleasant as they came on the bodies of the horses.

Fargo had Vera stay in camp with the boys when digging began again the next morning.

Her Conestoga proved to be badly smashed, the rear end and axle crushed. Later, Gabe Hazzard helped Vera return to collect her things. When dark descended and the evening meal was done, Fargo sat back and listened to Abel Gunnard address the others. "We have two wagons and enough horses to make a team for each. Those without a horse will ride the wagons. We'll make room. Vera and the boys will ride in with Hope. Harriet and I'll make room for anybody else who needs it," the man said. "I'm going to sleep now before I fall over. We'll work things out, come morning."

The others were quick to bed down. Fargo watched Hope go into the Conestoga with Vera and the boys, her face set, her round cheeks somehow drawn. He took his bedroll and started to the far side of the camp when Cassie appeared beside him. "I just want you to know I haven't forgotten any of what I said when you took me in, Fargo," she slid at him.

"I'll keep that in mind, honey," he said. She smiled as she moved away with her blanket. He crossed to the other side of the camp and settled down in the dampness of the night cold.

It had taken them four days, but they had two usable wagons and they'd be needed on every step of the way back. The dampness in the air was a warning, he frowned, but little Cassie was a promise. It would all be a balancing act, he knew, pleasure against pain, a race between bed and blizzard. He'd sure as hell try to win the first, and hope to avoid the second. He turned on his side and let weariness close out the night.

Abe Jones had made coffee in the early morning and Fargo gratefully sipped the hot and bracing brew, though it lacked the special touch Eb Story had given it. The cold wind swirled in gusts and the sun seemed to crawl over the high peaks. Gray, streaking clouds touched the farthest edges of the sky and Fargo waited for the others to emerge slowly and gather for coffee. He took them in with sweeping and firm glance. Only Hope was missing, still inside her Conestoga.

"I'll take you back, now," Fargo said, and drained his cup.

It was Abel Gunnard's voice that answered. "No," the man said softly.

Fargo felt astonishment curl inside him as he looked at Gunnard sitting on a rock, Harriet clinging to him. "No? Did you say no?" Fargo frowned. "Did I hear correctly?"

Gunnard looked uncomfortable but he held his ground. "You did. I'm going on," he said. He glanced up and met Fargo's stare of incredulousness.

"Dammit, man, you lost four days. That means you're four days closer to the first blizzard," Fargo said.

"I'm going on," Abel Gunnard repeated. "I have all my tools and enough men to work with me. It's still worth a try, maybe more than ever. I don't have anything to go back to. Going on is all I have left."

"You forgot one thing," Fargo snapped, and the man's eyes questioned. "Your life," Fargo rasped.

"I'm going on," Gunnard said with implacable doggedness.

Fargo looked at Harriet; her shrug was almost apologetic.

"Where Abel goes, I go," she said.

Fargo turned to Gabe Hazzard and his crew.

The man almost winced as he spoke. "We talked about it," he said. "We're not hankering to get ourselves killed, but maybe things won't be as bad as you keep saying. We took the job. We'll stay on, for a spell longer, at least."

Fargo turned to Vera and saw her haunted eyes churning with private depths. "I'm going on. I have to know. It was a sign," she said.

"What was a sign?" Fargo frowned.

"What happened back there, my being alive. It was a sign for me to go on, to find out. That's why I was spared, don't you see? I have to go on. I have to know!" Vera cried.

Fargo swore and spun on his heel to stalk away, but paused as he saw Hope standing beside the Conestoga. She had to have heard and he halted in front of her, his jaw a tight line, the question burning in his eyes. "Go on, say it," he rasped.

"I can't desert Vera. I have to go on with her," Hope murmured.

Fargo heard the bitter sound drop from his lips. "Jesus, what a lot," he muttered. "A man consumed with his dream of striking it rich; his woman, who stays because she knows she's nothing without him; a handful of hands with misplaced ideas about earning their hire; a woman captured by her own obsession; and you, a damn kettle of loyalty and self-punishment. I've had it with the whole damn lot of you. You can all go stew in your own juices."

He strode away, anger and frustration churning inside him. The sound of hurrying footsteps approached as Cassie ran to catch up to his long-legged strides. She halted with him at the far side of the camp where a tall spruce edged the main road of the pass.

"What are you going to do?" she asked, her light-blue eyes wide, her small face childlike.

"Get the hell out of here," Fargo barked. "I just might take Ted and Tim with me."

"Take them from their mother?" Cassie frowned.

"Why not? She's going to get them killed, only she won't believe it," Fargo returned angrily.

"Just doesn't seem right, somehow," Cassie said, and he grimaced at her words. She frowned into space for a moment more.

"They won't make it without you," she said matter-of-factly.

"Too bad. I'm not going along with their twisted, damn-fool craziness," Fargo said.

"Give them one more day to think it over," she said. "Give them a last chance. Tell them you'll give them the night to sleep on it, and then it's good-bye. Maybe when they realize you mean it, they'll change their minds. So far you've gone along with them each time. Let them know this is it."

Fargo frowned at her and felt his surprise at the reasoned wisdom in her words. She made sense, he realized, and his surprise turned to agreement. "All right, dammit, it might just work," he said. "And it'll give me some more time to think about what to do with the boys." Impulsively he hugged her to him. "You are a little package of surprises," he told her.

"Where are you bedding down tonight?" Cassie asked, her smile both seductive and shy.

"Soon as I find a place I'll be sure to tell you," he said.

"You going to take them on farther?" Cassie frowned.

"Yes, and I think I'll get a little help in changing their minds," he said. He swung onto the Ovaro and brought the horse back to where the others had started to gather, Vera sitting beside Hope on the Conestoga, Abe Jones at the tail of the big rack-bed, and two men riding alongside Abel. Ted and Tim sat their ponies.

The Trailsman halted and fixed Gunnard with a searing stare. "You've got tonight to change your fool minds. Sleep on it and come to your senses. If not, you're on your own tomorrow, and that's a promise."

Fargo swung the Ovaro away without waiting for a reply from anyone. He rode on up the pass but stayed not more than a few hundred yards ahead of the wagons, his eyes sweeping the high slopes that surrounded them. The pass had grown steeper and seemed to sprout side gullies and draws that flattened out in the midst of the high crags and granite slopes. High mountain northern pine and Canada balsam rose along the stone shouldered slopes.

When he spotted half a dozen ruffed grouse, the last they would see in this high country, he drew the Sharps and bagged four of the birds and hung them on the saddle horn with a piece of lariat.

He had ridden for a few hours when he halted. A single, near-naked horseman sat motionless on his mount on a nearby slope. Fargo stayed and let the wagons catch up to him.

Abel Gunnard followed his gaze up the slope. "Nez Percé?" Gunnard asked, and Fargo nodded. As he did so, the lone horseman backed his unshod mount into the trees and disappeared from sight.

"Move on," Fargo said, and spurred the pinto forward. They had gone almost another hour when Fargo slowed and gestured to the hill on the right where three Indians sat atop their mounts. He saw Gunnard and the others stare up at the three braves. Once again, the Indians moved back into the trees and vanished from sight. Fargo's lips pressed together tightly in a grim smile as he led the wagons forward.

An hour later, six Nez Percé warriors silently rested their ponies upon a high ledge. He saw Gabe Hazzard exchange nervous glances with Gunnard and frown as the Indians turned, almost as one, and slowly rode from the ledge to vanish into a passage between high rocks.

Fargo moved forward again. By now the sun had glided into the late afternoon, long shadows reaching down from the high crags. Suddenly the row of bronzed figures came into sight again. He counted nine this time and heard Abel's hoarse half-whisper.

"What the hell are they doing?" the man muttered.

"Making you nervous," Fargo said.

"Bastards," Gunnard spat. "You figure they'll come at us?"

"No, not this day," Fargo said. "They're being kind."

"Kind?" Gunnard echoed.

"They're letting you see them," Fargo said, and moved on.

The Nez Percé held their place this time, but two of them held lances, the rest with their short bows strung over one arm. He spurred the Ovaro into a trot and watched the bronzed figures finally turn and ride out of sight in the tall balsam that covered the high hill.

The pass grew steeper, but Fargo rode on through the darkening light until he spotted a place to camp where a half-circle of clear land edged a hill of thick white balsam and scrubby juniper. Abe Jones and one of the other men caught up to him first, and Jones immediately set to preparing the grouse for the roasting spit.

When Gunnard's wagon came into sight, the day had almost turned dark and the firelight danced in the dusk shadows. Hope drove in right behind Gunnard and Fargo frowned as he scanned the arrivals. "Where's Cassie?" he asked.

"She stopped back a ways. Her horse came down with a hobble," Hazzard said. "She told us to go on and she'd be along."

Fargo stepped onto the pass and stared down the pathway in the dim light still remaining. The creases deepened in his brow. The sky continued to darken. He was about to climb onto the Ovaro when he made out the horse coming up the path and, as it drew closer, Cassie's slim figure atop it. He peered at the horse when she reached him, halted, and slid from the saddle. "He seems to be moving all right," Fargo said.

"He had a small stone wedged in the frog. I used a piece of twig to finally get it out," she said, and walked beside him to where she tethered the horse on a low branch. He saw Hazzard standing beside Abel, both men scanning the almost dark hills.

"Don't waste your time. They've gone," Fargo said, and the two men turned back to the camp. When the meal was ready, he sat down and found Cassie beside him. Hope stayed with Vera and the others ate in total silence, he noted with satisfaction. The sight of the Nez Percé had done what he wanted it to do: added extra weight to his ultimatum. Maybe it'd tip the scales, he pondered. Not with Vera, of course. She was beyond reason and logic, possibly beyond fear. But not the others. They could still be reached. He was certain of one thing: they'd all think hard this night.

When he finished the meal, he handed the tin plate in as the others moved toward the wagons and prepared for bed. When Cassie appeared beside him, he smiled at her. "Up a few dozen yards in the spruce," he said, and she nodded with her own quick smile and hurried away.

He took down his bedroll and climbed the hillside under a moon that barely filtered through the thick spruce. He found a spot where the hill grew level for a few yards, and set his things down. Through a gap in the trees he could glimpse the ribbon that was the pass where it led from the camp. But as the moon slid behind a string of clouds, that too disappeared.

He shed his clothes quickly in the cold and slid into the warmth of his bedroll. He'd only stretched out when he heard the footsteps moving up the hillside, the cold-hardened ground making each step a softly distinct sound. The footsteps halted, then moved on again with aimless uncertainty.

"Up here," he called softly. The footsteps quickened at once and Cassie's small shape appeared. She carried the wool, three-quarter-length jacket in one hand and shivered as she reached him, but as he held the bedroll open, she flung the one-piece dress over her head and once again became the lithe, slender wood nymph he had seen that first morning.

With graceful quickness she lowered herself into the bedroll, her arms around his neck at once, hugging his warmth to her. When she relaxed her grip, he took in her loveliness—everything small yet perfectly balanced. She had beautifully shaped breasts with light-pink tips— miniature breasts, he thought—a flat abdomen, and a small, very black triangle, narrow hips, and thin legs. Cassie was, he decided, jewellike, but with a warm, sensuous sparkle instead of cold brilliance.

His hand reached out and lightly caressed one small breast. Cassie cried out with pleasure. "Oh, yes, oh, nice," she breathed, pushing herself upward. He brought his face down to the little white mounds, passed his lips from one light-pink tip to the next and back again as Cassie sighed in delight. When he took one minia-ture breast into his mouth, her hands became fists and drummed against his shoulders.

His tongue curled around the tiny tip and Cassie cried out, her thin legs moving up and down against each other. "Jesus . . . oh, God," she murmured, and the words turned into a long, sibilant sigh when he let his hand slowly move down along her body, pressing gently, pausing to explore the little black triangle. "Uuuuuh," Cassie sighed. Her legs stiffened and she dug her heels into the ground and pushed her pelvis upward.

Fargo brought his hand down farther to cup the dark, warm moistness, and Cassie half-screamed at his touch. He held her for a moment, then moved to smooth his hand over the lubricious lips. "Yes, yes . . . ah, ah, ah, take me, take me," Cassie gasped, her narrow hips twisting from side to side. But Fargo waited, caressing her moist, small darkness as she cried out in delight.

He waited, watching her small body quiver and her hands clutching at him. Her light-blue eyes stared with pleading until he brought himself over her, let his hotly throbbing organ press down on the small pubic mound. "Oh, nice . . . nice, oh, oh." She pulled and pushed at him until he moved down, his throbbing maleness against her, slowly pushing forward. Cassie cried out, pain and pleasure in the sound, and he remembered what she told him. He moved slowly, gently, felt her tightness give way and a groaning sigh erupt from her. He paused, rested, and let her throbbing surround him.

"More, more," Cassie gasped. He drew back, thrust forward, and completely filled her. She screamed again, a quick gasp of pain, then a long sighing cry of delight. "Again, oh, again . . . oh, yes, yes," she murmured, and Fargo began to move inside her, forcing short cries of pleasure with every slow thrust.

It was plain that she'd told the truth about the others. This was the first time for her, and her absolute enjoyment reached out to him, pulled him along with new excitement. Suddenly Cassie's wood-sprite body quivered, then quickly grew taut. Her pelvis arched upward and he supported her, one hand encircling the small waist. She offered the miniature breasts up to his lips. "Take me . . . take them . . . oh, God, please," she cried out, and he drew one tiny mound into his mouth as she exploded. She screamed, a cry of discovery and delight, and her arms circled his neck, her body pressed tight against his.

Even as she grew still, the moment of ecstasy slipping away, she clung tightly to him. He lay down with her and she curled around him, legs and arms locked in an embrace of flesh to flesh. He enjoyed her clinging warmth, the way she pressed herself to him with a combination of childlike sweetness and womanly sensuality.

He was still holding her when the scream came through the night, a woman's voice, and Fargo felt his muscles tighten. He tried to sit up but Cassie still clung with all her might. The scream sounded again. With a curse, he rolled, flung Cassie away from him, and leapt to his feet. He heard a horse galloping by as he yanked on Levi's.

Colt in hand, he raced down the hillside. Now there were shouts from the camp, voices raised in alarm. When he reached the wagons, he saw Abel Gunnard hurrying to the Conestoga. Gabe Hazzard was already at the wagon where Hope held Vera and helped lift her to her feet. "They took the boys," Hope said, and Fargo saw the smear of blood on Vera's temple.

"Who?" Fargo barked. "The Nez Percé?"

"No, those two fat men you wouldn't let come along," Hope said.

"Ma Cowley's spawn," Gunnard said.

"Zeb and Zane," Fargo muttered.

"When we woke, they were inside the wagon," Hope said. "I heard horses a little while before and thought they were ours. Vera went at them, but they hit her and grabbed Ted and Tim. I tried to stop them, but they threw me out of the wagon."

Fargo stared down the blackness of the pass. There would be no way to pick up their tracks until morning, if then. But he felt another fury spiraling inside him, pushing aside all else as it filled him with a towering rage. He turned and saw the small figure come into view. She had the wool jacket on now and walked quietly, almost deliberately, toward her horse. Fargo, his mouth a thin line, was at her in three long strides, and his arms shot out as if with a will of their own, his hands closing around her thin neck. He lifted her off her feet as he would a doll.

"Goddamn you," he hissed. "Goddamn you." She only stared back with her light-blue eyes expressionless. "Bitch. Stinking little bitch. You did it to me again. The same but different." He watched Cassie's eyes begin to bulge as her breath became a mere trickle of air. His arms trembled and he knew he wanted to squeeze harder, fling her lying little body against a tree trunk and smash it into bits.

"Damn you. Damn your rotten, stinking hide," he hissed. Cassie's face had begun to turn ashen; her lips opened but only a gasp of air came from them. His entire body still trembled with rage, fury fighting against itself, but he forced his hands open and dropped her to the ground. Reason had pounded its way through rage. If she had any value to him it was alive, not dead. Payment could wait. Justice would find a time.

He put the toe of his foot under her rear as she sat

rubbing her neck with one hand, lifted, and sent her sprawling. "Get up, damn you," he barked, and she pushed to her feet, her small face holding a half-pout.

"I do what Ma Cowley tells me to do," Cassie said.

"Not anymore you won't," Fargo rasped, and turned to Gabe Hazzard. "Put a rope collar around her neck and tie her wrists behind her back. Then tether her to a tree with her blanket."

The man moved quickly and Fargo turned to where Hope speared him with icy disdain. "She kept you too busy to hear anything you might have heard until it was too late," Hope bit out.

"I never figured it for that," Fargo said.

"You just keep on being eager, don't you?" she sniffed.

He swore silently and groped for an answer when the sound of a wagon broke into his thoughts. He turned to the road to see the high-sided farm wagon bouncing along behind the hard-running team, the mountainous figure at the reins. The wagon rolled into the campsite and braked to a halt as Ma Cowley picked up the rifle on her lap. "Now everybody stay calm," the huge woman rasped, her small eyes scanning the campsite with cold confidence.

Fargo saw Vera burst from the Conestoga, leap to the ground, and race toward Ma Cowley's wagon.

"Where are my boys?" Vera screamed. "Give me my boys." She reached the wagon and had started to climb aboard when Fargo saw Ma Cowley raise the rifle butt. He moved with the speed of silent lightning, curled his arm around Vera's waist, and pulled her from the wagon before the beastly woman smashed the rifle butt into her face. Vera struggled to get free but Fargo held her in place.

"Stop it," he growled, and shook her for a moment. "That won't get you anything but a cracked head."

"Now, that's good advice, girlie," Ma Cowley said, and swept the others with her small eyes snapping. "You'll be taking orders from me from now on, especially you, Fargo, if you want to see those kids alive again." She paused, fastening her eyes on Fargo where he stood with Hope beside him. "Anything happens to me, those kids are dead. You understand, Fargo?" she growled.

"I hear you," he said, spitting out the words.

"You're going to be taking us through Blood Pass," the hag croaked.

"The Nez Percé won't let that happen," Fargo answered.

"You find a way or else," she said, and moved her wagon to one side. She lowered her mountainous bulk to the ground, swinging backward from the driver's seat. "Now we're all going to get some sleep, and come morning, we'll move on," she said, and beckoned to Cassie. "You sleep in the wagon with me, dearie," she hissed.

Cassie obediently moved toward her with a glance back at Fargo.

Damn, he fumed as he turned away. She managed to look helpless, even innocent. The mask was built into her, the way some people were born with a tic or a birthmark, he raged silently. She disappeared into the high-sided wagon and Ma Cowley followed, clambering in through the tailgate, the folds of the tentlike dress billowing out.

Fargo started to turn away but Hope's hand reached out and caught his arm. "There must be something we can do," she said.

"We can do what she says and keep the boys alive," Fargo said harshly. "She's arranged some way to let her two dim-witted offspring know if something goes wrong here. Until I find out how and what, we can't move against her. Zeb and Zane have orders to kill the boys, and they'll do it." He saw Hope hold her eyes closed for a moment, gather strength inside, and pull them open again.

"Look on the bright side," Fargo said. "You're getting what you wanted." She frowned back at him. "You wanted me to keep taking you on. It looks as though I'm going to be doing that." He strode away, the bitterness in his voice still hanging in the air.

Back on the hillside of spruce, he crawled into his bedroll. He drew it tight against the cold and swore in frustration. Everything had changed. In one sudden moment when treachery was cloaked in ecstasy, it had all changed. He found himself wondering how Ma Cowley had known this night was the one Cassie would bed him down. Perhaps it had all been prearranged, a certain number of nights counted off when Cassie would do her thing. But he frowned at the explanation. What if the Nez Percé had changed the routine? What if he'd had to stand sentry, unavailable for Cassie's charms? Zeb and Zane would have ridden up and been seen, the entire scheme exposed. Had that simply been a risk she had no choice but to take? He grimaced and knew it was possible, but it didn't satisfy. It was too hit-and-miss, and the woman had planned and waited. No, there'd been something else, he grunted. He'd have to bide his time and watch, though he knew there was little time left. Another few days would put them close to the top of Blood Pass—and the Nez Percé burial grounds. The Indians wouldn't wait for them to desecrate that sacred land. He turned on his side and drew sleep around him, a refuge from what was beginning to seem an inexorable march to death.

When morning came and he rose, washed, and dressed, he found Ma Cowley having coffee, Cassie dwarfed beside her massive bulk. Abel Gunnard and the others sipped their coffee in a small cluster. Abe Jones handed Fargo a tin cup.

"I'll be lead wagon," Ma said. "You go and ride ahead just as if nothin's been changed, Fargo."

His eyes were hard as he peered over the rim of the tin cup at the woman. "What makes you so all-fired anxious to go through Blood Pass?" he questioned.

"Can't go around the mountains. Too many sheriffs out looking for us," Ma Cowley said. "But we'll be in new territory when we come out the other side of the pass, no sheriffs to bother about."

"What else?" Fargo growled.

"That's it," the woman bristled.

"Bullshit," Fargo shot back. "Sheriffs will jail you. The Nez Percé will bury you. There's more. What else are you running from?"

The huge woman's small eyes grew smaller. "Real smartass you are," she muttered, and Fargo shrugged.

"The way you tell, it doesn't add up," he said.

"There was a man. He was killed, an accident, we didn't mean to kill him," Ma Cowley said. "But he was the governor's assistant. There's a hanging warrant out for us. It won't carry the other side of Blood Pass."

Fargo nodded and finished his coffee. The truth usually made sense. He handed Abe Jones his cup and swung onto the Ovaro. As the others climbed into their wagons, he took his horse onto the pass and rode northwest along the road. He didn't hurry as the pass rose in front of him, a ribbon between sides of tall ponderosa pine. He scanned the surrounding high land but saw no sign of the Nez Percé. But they were there, he was certain, waiting and watching.

He had just crested over the top of the steep rise where it leveled off when he pulled to a halt. He stared at the lance that had been plunged into the middle of the road, a lone white-and-brown eagle feather bound to the top of it.

Fargo kept the Ovaro in one place and saw that the sun had slipped past the noon sky when the wagons rolled to a stop behind him. Hope peered out from behind Gunnard's rig, her eyes on the lance embedded in the ground.

"What's that supposed to mean?" Ma Cowley called out.

"A sign. They're telling you not to go any farther," Fargo said.

"Pull it out," the woman ordered.

"You want it out, you do it," Fargo said.

"You afraid to pull it out?" Ma Cowley barked.

"Afraid's not the word, but I'm not pulling it out," Fargo said.

"Afraid is the word, goddamn you," Ma Cowley roared, and turned on Abel Gunnard. "You want to go through the pass, don't you?" she roared, and he nodded through his uneasiness. "You pull it out."

Abel Gunnard started to climb down from his wagon.

"Leave it alone," Fargo said.

"Shut up," Ma Cowley roared. "I'm giving the orders around here."

Fargo's eyes held Gunnard and the man shifted uncertainly. "Stay on your wagon," Fargo said, his voice ice-hard. Gunnard sat back on the seat beside Harriet. Fargo turned to Ma Cowley. "You want it out, you do it," he growled.

"Goddamn cowards, all of you," the huge woman said, and lurched down from her wagon with surprising speed. As Cassie stayed back atop her horse, Ma Cowley strode to the lance and yanked it from the ground. With a curse, she flung it down and stomped on it, kicked it aside, and strode back to her wagon. Fargo's eyes were scanning the hills when she climbed back onto the driver's seat of her wagon. Twelve near-naked horsemen appeared as if by magic, six on one side of the pass, six on the other. They moved down slowly, deliberately, and came to a halt to stand silently, as if sculptured of granite.

"What are they going to do, come at us?" Fargo heard Gabe Hazzard ask, dismay in his voice.

"No," Fargo said. "They'll look, count, take us in the way a hawk takes in a chicken yard. Then they'll leave. For now."

As though the Indians had heard his words, they turned slowly and moved back up the hillsides until they vanished into the spruce.

"Let's get the hell on," Ma Cowley rasped.

Fargo moved forward, put the pinto into a trot, and left the others behind. He hurried beneath the afternoon sky and slowed where the pass climbed in a succession of short, steep rises and equally short flat places. When he halted, his gaze moved to the left where a narrow pathway, wide enough for only a single rider, cut through a dense forest of Canada balsam. It was a dark passage, the giant trees hanging densely and forbiddingly over the narrow opening, but it was a passage he knew. He had ridden it before and memories slid through his mind with a grim kind of fondness. He turned away, rode on another hundred yards, and pulled off the pass into a glen of heavy-scented northern pine.

Dusk blanketed the mountains when the others rolled up and pulled the three wagons to the sides of the glen. As Abe Jones prepared a fast meal of dried beef strips and beans, Fargo saw Harriet come toward him, her eyes searching his face.

"You had a reason for telling Abel not to pull out the lance," she said.

"The Nez Percé make special note of whoever pulls out the lance," Fargo said. "Special note for a special answer."

"Thank you," Harriet murmured, and her hand closed around his arm.

"For what it's worth," Fargo said bitterly.

Abe Jones called everyone to the fire and Ma Cowley and Cassie came together. When the meal was finished, the huge woman rose and scanned the gathering.

"You're all scared shitless by a few damn Indians," she said.

"Scared's better than stupid," Fargo said. "There'll be a lot more, come tomorrow."

"It won't mean anything because you're going to visit your friend the chief," the woman said. "You're gonna talk to him about us going through."

"It'll be a waste of time," Fargo said. "He'll never agree."

"I heard he owes you," Ma Cowley said.

"Not that much, not in his eyes," Fargo told her.

"You go talk to him, come morning. You get him to let us through," Ma Cowley said. "No more arguing over it." She climbed into her wagon and Cassie followed with childlike obedience.

Abel Gunnard, Hope, and Vera stood beside Fargo, watching him with a mixture of fear and hope in their eyes.

"It's worth a try," Gunnard ventured.

"Maybe, but not for any of the reasons you're thinking," Fargo answered harshly.

Gunnard turned away and retired into his wagon. Vera left on silent steps and only Hope remained, her round-cheeked face grave.

"What reasons?" she asked. "You have a plan."

"Plan?" Fargo almost laughed the word. "I've got some stray thoughts. Maybe they'll turn into something more. Maybe they won't."

She continued to peer beyond the reply, but finally gave up and went into the Conestoga.

Fargo took down his bedroll and slid into its warmth on the far side of the camp. He hadn't lied to her. He had no plan. But he would do anything he could to buy time, time to formulate a plan. Freeing Ted and Tim was still the key to everything else, and to do that he had to find out how Ma Cowley kept in touch with her two oaf sons.

Time, he murmured as he closed his eyes. How much was there left to buy? he wondered before sleep closed away further thoughts.

6

Morning crept gray across the sky, and the cold wind bit hard as he woke. Ma Cowley emerged from her wagon with Cassie in tow. The woman came toward him as he finished the cup of coffee Abe Jones had brewed.

"You ready to go?" Ma Cowley growled. Fargo saw the others emerge from their wagons. He nodded and drained the coffee. "I'm sending Cassie along," the huge woman said.

"What the hell for?" Fargo flared. "She's not going to help me any by coming along."

"You could come back and tell me anything," the woman said. "Cassie's going along to keep you honest. She'll tell me the truth."

Fargo's eyes were ice-blue as he stared at the woman and silently cursed her cunning cleverness. His hands curled into fists as he fought the urge to sink one into the middle of that mountain of fat. But Ma Cowley still held two hole cards and they both knew it.

He turned away and swung himself onto the Ovaro and waited as Cassie half-ran to her horse and rode up beside him, her light-blue eyes still innocently wide. He swept the high ridges with a quick glance before he rode from the glen. Two silent bronzed figures on their ponies looked down from atop a ledge. He knew their eyes followed him as he rode onto the pass, back a hundred yards or so, and turned into the narrow passage between the tall ponderosa pine.

Cassie swung in behind him, rode close on his heels as he moved down the narrow passageway. Only when the passage widened and the trees grew less thick did she have an opportunity to come up beside him again.

"It was good the other night," she said. "I liked it a lot."

Fargo glanced at her and felt incredulity taking over again. She looked at him as though nothing else had happened. "That supposed to make me feel good about it?" he tossed at her.

"I didn't lie to you. It was my first time." She half-shrugged.

"That's the only thing you didn't lie about," Fargo snapped. "I'll be dammed if I understand you."

"I still liked it," she said almost offhandedly, riding along with placid, unfazed ease.

Little Cassie, he decided, was made of separate pieces that stayed apart from one another, never connecting to make up a whole. It let her lead a compartmental life where innocence and betrayal could exist side by side.

He was still regarding her with amazement when the horsemen came from the trees in front of him and Fargo reined to a halt. Six of them, he counted, the one in front wearing a piece of shale piercing one nostril. They wore only loincloths. They were young, stern-faced; their black eyes filled with suspicion. Though the Nez Percé spoke the Shahaptian language, most spoke enough Shoshone to communicate with the neighboring tribes, so Fargo used the Shoshone, which he knew best.

"I come to see Walking Deer," he said. "I am old friend." He used sign language for the last phrase.

The Indian thought for a moment, then beckoned for him to follow. Fargo swung in behind the six braves, Cassie beside him. Four more bronzed forms moved through the trees on each side.

He smelled the camp before they reached it, bear meat cooking, hides still drying, pine wood burning. "From here on I do all the talking," Fargo told Cassie, who nodded. He detected lines of fear in her small face and was glad. Fear would keep her quiet. The terrain grew wider until it opened into a deep gulley where six tepees clustered near one another, three campfires burning. A hide-drying rack rested near one fire and a half-dozen squaws were fashioning bundles of twigs. As he was led into the camp, the largest tepee in front of him, he saw others emerge from their tents to gaze at him and the small, blond creature beside him. The tent flap of the largest tepee opened and a tall, thin man stepped outside, three eagle feathers in his hair, a two-piece hide garment clothing his body.

Fargo scanned the long, lined face, much as he remembered it with perhaps a few added crow's feet around the almond-shaped eyes.

"It has been a long time, Fargo," the chief said. "But time does not wipe away memory." He spoke the Shoshone dialect.

Fargo climbed down from the Ovaro. "Walking Deer is still the great chief of the mountain Nez Percé," Fargo said. He nodded to Cassie, almost a gesture of dismissal. "This is my woman," he said. The Nez Percé chief didn't even glance at her.

"You are with those who come closer each day to the top of Blood Pass, Fargo. Why?" Walking Deer questioned.

"They have not listened to me," Fargo said, and the Indian nodded in understanding. "They have asked me to come to you, to tell you to let them cross the pass."

"You know that is impossible, Fargo," the chief said sternly. "Our guards stand on the sacred ground. No one can cross."

"And if they go on?" Fargo pressed.

"We will make the ground red with their blood. But you know that, Fargo, and you know why," Walking Deer answered.

"I know that, but they wanted me to bring back your words," Fargo said.

"I do not want to see your blood on the leaves of the pass, old friend. But you know I will have no choice." There was sadness in the Nez Percé chief's voice.

"I know." Fargo nodded.

"We make ready for the long snows. You should leave the pass, Fargo, before you are trapped," the Indian said.

"I'll bring them your words," Fargo said. "May the gods of the Nez Percé embrace their people."

"May you live to visit again one day, Fargo," the chief said, a second layer of meaning beneath the words.

Fargo started to mount the pinto and paused. "I may need time. Will you wait, old friend?" he asked.

"For you, Fargo," the chief said, and stayed outside his tepee until Fargo rode from the camp, Cassie a few paces at his heels.

When the Indian camp was out of sight and the narrow passageway came into view, Fargo waved her alongside him. "You hear enough?" he asked harshly.

"It's not up to me," Cassie said.

"You just say what you heard," Fargo growled, and fell silent as he started through the narrow passage. He had bought a little more time and that was all-important, an extra day, an extra night, another moment to watch, think, plan.

He rode slowly, wrapped in his own thoughts. Ma Cowley and her two oafish sons holding Ted and Tim were still the key players. They still contacted one another in some way, and he had to find out how. Without that, without finding a way to save the boys, he was a man with his hands tied. Thoughts continued to whirl through his mind, probes he held aside and some he discarded. When he finally came in sight of the glen, he still had nothing concrete.

The others came forward at once as he rode in with Cassie, Vera springing from the Conestoga, Ma Cowley standing implacably beside her wagon. Fargo dismounted and told them what the Nez Percé chief had said, harsh satisfaction in his voice mixed with contempt.

When he finished, Ma Cowley turned to Cassie. "He telling it like it was?" the woman asked.

Cassie nodded. "Only there was something more," she added, and Fargo turned to frown at her. "They're not all up there. They've sentries posted, nothing more," Cassie said, and Ma Cowley's smile seemed to take minutes to spread across her wide face.

"Good. Very good, dearie. We get rid of the sentries and go on through," the woman said.

"They'll know. They'll find them and come after you," Fargo said.

"We'll be on our way. Let them chase us," Ma Cowley said. "We're going on through." Her eyes went to Fargo, suddenly cold as ice. "You'll take their sentries, Fargo. That'll be your job. Take anybody you need with you, but kill those sentries."

"If I say no?" Fargo asked.

"Those two kids are dead," the woman snapped.

Fargo let the hate in his eyes spear into her, but Ma Cowley shrugged it away. "You let them go and I'll take care of the guards for you," he countered.

Her laugh was a harsh, twisted sound. "Sure you will. You must take me for a goddamn fool," she snarled.

"I give my word, I keep it," he said.

"The only word I trust is my own," the woman snarled. "Those guards or the kids. Your choice, Fargo."

Fargo felt Vera's eyes burning into him. He cast a glance at Hope. She waited, hands clenched together, lips parted, anguish in her face. His eyes snapped back to Ma Cowley. "The guards," he growled.

Her lips curled in triumph. "Now, that's being real smart," she said, and turned to Abe Jones. "Get supper started. I'm hungry," she grumbled.

Fargo's smile was cloaked in grimness. Again, he'd bought time. She'd pay him little attention now, certain he'd concentrate all his energies on the task that lay ahead of him. He'd given her the victory. There was nothing like winning to breed overconfidence. He started to walk away with the Ovaro in the lowering dusk when Hope crossed to meet him.

"Thank you for what you're doing for the boys," she said. "Maybe it'll be best for everybody."

"Hope dies hard, doesn't it?" Fargo muttered, and she shrugged, helplessness in the gesture. He frowned down at her and anger blazed in his eyes, his words barely audible. "I agreed only because right now she's got me trapped. I don't do what she says and she kills the boys. I do what she wants and the Nez Percé kill all of us. That's the truth of it and you better face it, dammit."

"You're saying there's no hope, no way out," she answered.

"While there's time, there's hope," Fargo said, and went on, pulling the horse behind him. He sat down alone and watched the others gather around the cookfire. The dampness was heavy in the night air again, and Fargo swore softly. He'd bought time from Walking Tree and from Ma Cowley, but there'd be no buying time from Mother Nature. When the cooking was finished, he took his meal off by himself and the others ate in silence, occupied with their own thoughts. They all still clung to their hopes, he knew, some out of their dreams of glory, some out of obsession, some because there was nothing left but hope. And he was left with the cold specter of reality and questions he couldn't answer.

He finished the last of his food and swallowed it in sourness, watched Cassie follow the hulking figure of Ma Cowley into the wagon. He took his bedroll into the trees and drew sleep to him, only to have it a restless blanket. He was awake, thoughts churning inside him, when dawn broke. He rose, washed, and saw the sun light its way through more than morning grayness. The damp cold stabbed at him. But his tossing thoughts had brought no answers, and when the others rose, he led the way north up the pass. He saw the silent, watching horsemen in the high hills as he rode, keeping pace with the wagons that rolled along slowly behind. Walking Tree had promised he'd wait, and Fargo trusted the Indian's word. But the wagons would be near the top of Blood Pass in another day, perhaps two. How close dared he come to that sacred ground before the Nez Percé went into action? he wondered. The chief had drawn no line. Would he wait until the very last moment? Would he tell his warriors the distance was to be measured in hours or in days? Fargo grimaced at the thought. It was one more question for which he had no answer, one more tinderbox waiting to explode in his face.

The wind whipped with a new cold in it and the sun stayed weak until the day's end. The ponderosa pine and northern spruce had given ground to tall, thin tamaracks, and the cold whistled down from the high crags. He had halted at a high stream and waited for the wagons to come up, his eyes searching for Ma Cowley. The woman bristled with smug confidence, certain she had things well in hand. He silently cursed her smugness and stupidity. He had let thoughts tumble back and forth through his mind all day, waiting for something to strike a spark. But the spark never flared and now he stretched out in weariness when night fell. He'd have to change his approach. He'd been searching too hard, seeking in too many directions, he reprimanded himself. But not until morning when his mind would be fresh again. He closed his eyes and slept quickly and soundly.

Morning came with the sky gray and the wind cold. The Trailsman rose, dressed, and swept the crags with a quick glance. He saw two Nez Percé warriors, standing their horses as if they were part of the rocks. When the others were ready to move out, Fargo sent the pinto up the pass where a terrain of small, windswept pebbles became a road. Again, the Nez Percé moved with them in the high rocks and Fargo felt the apprehension stab at him. They'd be drawing close to the top of Blood Pass by tomorrow. Would this be their last day? he had to ask himself. He ought to call a halt here and now, he knew, but Ma Cowley would never stand for it and she still held the hole cards.

He pushed aside further wonderings and concentrated on the one thing that could save them but continued to stay shrouded in its own cloak. Yet he couldn't afford another wasted day of thoughts racing freely, of waiting for something that might never catch fire. He had to concentrate on each step, try to reconstruct each single thing the woman had managed to do. First was sending Zeb and Zane on the right night, her certainty that Cassie would be using her passionate deceit. How had she been sure? How had she known? The answer had to involve Cassie, somehow, and as the morning wore into afternoon he refused to let his thoughts skip to anything else. Moment by moment, he went over everything that had happened that day, everything he had done, everything he'd seen the others do. Suddenly his brow furrowed. He had been far ahead of the wagons that day, as he was every day. He didn't really know what had taken place behind him during most of the long day. He certainly didn't know what Cassie had done for most of it, and Fargo suddenly reined to a halt.

The groove dug deeper into his brow as his thoughts leapt backward. Cassie had come into the camp last. Her horse had developed a hobble and she'd had to fall behind, a rock in the frog of the hoof, he remembered her explaining when she'd finally ridden up. But she had lagged behind at least a half-hour. A surge of excitement welled in him. Little Cassie had lagged behind that day and she could have lagged behind any number of times during any of the days. If they were for short periods, the others probably hadn't even noticed.

But, Fargo frowned, short periods wouldn't give her time to make contact with Ma Cowley. The woman hadn't been following close enough for that, or he'd have detected her. Yet something had gone on, he was certain of that much, and his thoughts raced on as he looked back at Cassie riding beside the three wagons, Gabe Hazzard and his men on the other side. She'd done no lagging behind this day. He'd been in constant sight of the wagons the entire day and she'd stayed with the others. Because he'd been too close, Fargo mused. He'd follow through on that, he decided. If Cassie was the key to all of it, if she'd somehow, someway, managed to make contact with Zeb and Zane each day, she'd have to do something before this day was finished. If indeed it had been her. That was still all speculation. Or perhaps only a desperate grasp at a straw in the wind, he reminded himself.

He continued to move up the pass and finally drew to a halt as the purple gray of dusk began to slide across the mountains. He peered ahead, his jaw set tight. He dared go no farther, not without knowing what he had to know. The top of Blood Pass and its sacred Nez Percé ground lay but another few hours away. The Nez Percé would never let them draw more than another hour closer, he was certain, and he'd no wish to face that until morning. His gaze swept the high mountain land that bordered the pass where he had halted. The terrain opened to a series of mountain gullies and draws that cut through the crags. He imprinted the land on his mind before settling on a narrow stretch alongside the main pass.

The wagons rolled up and he waved them into the narrow strip of land, hanging back and watching Cassie ride past alongside Ma Cowley's high-sided farm wagon. When the others settled in, he dismounted, his eyes still on Cassie. He'd keep his eyes on her, he grunted, stay with his speculation. Perhaps it was only that straw in the wind, he admitted, but he had no choice. It was more than he'd had up to now. He tethered the Ovaro at the far side of the rock-lined space.

"We're about at the last of the beans and beef strips," Abe Jones said. "We'll have to shoot us some fresh game in another day."

"Unless this is going to be our last supper," Fargo said with bitterness. He sat alone, finished his plate, and had started for the deep shadows with his bedroll when Hope came to him. Her round-cheeked prettiness seemed more out of place than ever in the bleakness of this high mountain land.

"There are a lot of things I'm sorry for," she said gravely. "I just wanted you to know that."

"The things that happened or the things that didn't happen?" he asked.

"Both," she murmured.

"Words like that could come back if there's a tomorrow." Fargo half-laughed.

"Will there be a tomorrow?" Hope asked.

"If you turn back. Nothing's changed there," he said.

"I know," she murmured sadly, and slowly walked from him.

He watched her reach the wagon and climb inside as the last of the fire smoldered to an end. He lay down in his bedroll in the deep shadows against the rocks and stretched, relaxing his body as he prepared to wait. If the straw he waited for turned out to be right, tomorrow might yet rescue them from the brink of doom. But time was running out, its measure no longer days but hours and, all too soon, minutes. His lips a thin line, he lay still, his eyes fixed on Cassie's sleeping form in the black shadows against the rocks of the narrow strip of land.

The moon, a hardly visible, fuzzy sphere through the clouds, barely lighted the pass as the night grew still, the camp asleep. Fargo blinked his eyes, pressed them tight, and snapped them open, and the tentative fingers of somnolence fled at once. He stayed unmoving when the blackness of the shadows seemed to stir and then the small, slim figure appeared, crossing to where her horse was tied.

Fargo watched her lead the horse onto the pass into the darkness. He waited, then rose slowly and went to the Ovaro. Cassie would not mount up until she was far enough away, so he gave her the chance to put distance between them before he swung onto the Ovaro. He followed, keeping the horse at a slow trot and straining his wild-creature hearing, until he picked up the sound of her horse. She'd gone into a trot, and he followed, closing distance carefully. He drew the Ovaro to the side of the pass and heard her slow. He reined up at once and dropped to the ground on the balls of his feet, leaving the Ovaro behind a tall spruce and hurrying forward, his long frame bent over in a half-crouch.

She had halted, only silence drifting back to him, so he stayed against the side of the pass as he moved forward. He peered through the darkness when the sound of hoofbeats suddenly exploded, and he managed to see the dark shape of the horse racing back toward him. Fargo dropped flat against the side of the road as she went by, riding fast. He lay still until the sounds of her hoofbeats faded away. He rose, a frown pulling his face, and hurried down the pass. She hadn't just stopped and turned around to race back, an exercise in the night. He wondered if she'd met someone and promptly discarded the thought. He would have heard other hoofbeats. He brought himself to a halt as only the darkness of the pass stretched out ahead. Damn, had he missed something? He swore and dropped to one knee to run his fingers across the soil of the pass as he peered down at the hard, dry ground. She hadn't come this far, he determined, and he stayed on his knees as he started to make his way back, running his fingers across the ground with each step.

He froze as he felt the indentations of the hoofprints, and rose to his feet. She had stopped here. He turned slowly and peered at the trees that grew to the edge of the path. There was a rush of surprise in his breath as he spotted the piece of fabric stuck on the end of a low branch. He stepped to it, touched it with one hand. Cotton, he murmured, a torn piece of blouse. It was a signal. It had a meaning. And they'd have to find it to get that meaning, Fargo muttered as he made his way through the spruce and sank down on one knee in the black depths of the trees.

The wait was short. The horses approached slowly. The two riders finally came into sight. Even the night could not hide their paunches as they moved their horses in slow steps until the one nearest him reined to a halt.

"There," he said. Fargo heard Zeb's voice. The man reached out and snatched the piece of cotton from the branch and waved it at Zane.

"Those two little bastards are lucky," Zane said. "We didn't find it this trip they'd be dead."

"Wonder what took her so long today?" Zeb said.

"Who knows? It's there. We found it, so everything's all right," Zane said. "Let's get back."

They turned their horses and started to ride unhurriedly away.

Fargo left his hiding place in the thick spruce and began to follow. He fell into the long, loping stride that let him devour ground effortlessly. He moved after the two horses as a wolf follows its prey—unseen, silent, a dogged shadow of death. Even when the two men put their horses into a trot, he followed, increasing the length of his loping strides. They were completely unaware of his presence as they turned from the pass and went into a clearing walled in on three sides with rock. Fargo dropped to one knee and watched them dismount, scanning the small clearing with a harsh glance, then halting when he spotted the two small figures tied together.

He waited, gathering his thoughts along with his breath. Cassie had left a piece of the torn cotton blouse each day, finding a way to fall back far enough to leave the signal. No signal meant that things had gone wrong and they were to follow the plan already

123

set. That explained how Ma Cowley knew the exact night Cassie would work her charms in his bedroll. Cassie had left the signal for her; Fargo's anger spiraled instantly at the thought of his betrayal.

His breath returned when he saw Zeb and Zane starting to put their blankets down. Fargo rose to a crouch. He had to take them in silence. Gunshots could carry far through the night mountains, to Nez Percé ears and, even more important at the moment, to Ma Cowley. It would give the woman a chance to take someone else as a hostage or, realizing what had happened, erupt in a rampage of killing. No shots, he told himself again, and began to move forward.

The two oafish hulks were very protective of each other. He'd make use of that to keep them from drawing and getting off at least two shots. He moved into the small clearing on silent steps; Tim's eyes widened as the boy saw him. Fargo put a finger to his lips and crept forward to where Zeb was making small snorting noises as he slept, his fat paunch quivering. Fargo drew his Colt, halted beside the man, and knelt down beside him. He put the barrel of the revolver against Zeb's temple, pressed, and the man woke instantly.

"One wrong move and you're dead, you hear me?" Fargo said. He reached down and pulled the six-gun from Zeb's holster.

Zeb stared at him, blinked his small eyes. "Zane," he called out with almost childlike alarm, and Fargo saw the other man sit up at once.

"Son of a bitch," Zane muttered. "What are you doing here?"

"Getting ready to blow his brains all over these mountains," Fargo said.

Zane stared at him, his small eyes filled with racing thoughts.

"Don't let him do that, Zane," Zeb cried out in fear.

"Throw your gun over here," Fargo barked. "Take

it out with two fingers and throw it over here." He pulled the hammer back on the Colt and the soft click sounded as though it were a cannon in the small stone-lined space.

Zane carefully lifted his gun from its holster and threw it across the ground. Fargo stepped back, scooped up both guns, and emptied the shells from each. Backing away, he stopped beside the two boys and drew the double-edged knife from his calf holster. He severed the ropes that tied the boys, but his gaze was still locked on Zeb and Zane, who pulled their paunchy, heavy bodies upright and glowered at him.

Ted and Tim leaped up and clung to Fargo's legs. "You'll be all right now," he said soothingly. "Just back off until I take care of these two."

Ted and Tim quickly pulled their arms from him and stepped away.

"You gonna shoot us?" Zeb asked in his almost childlike manner.

"No, I'm going to tie you up and keep you out of trouble," Fargo answered. He glanced at their horses and saw the lariat hanging from the strap of the nearest mount. He started toward it when Zane's voice interrupted.

"Why ain't you gonna shoot us?" the man asked, and Fargo saw the craftiness in the small eyes as he waited for an answer.

"I'm feeling kindly tonight," Fargo said, but he saw the craftiness turn to cunning. Perhaps they were dullards, oafs on the down side of ordinary intelligence, yet they had their own puerile acumen, and he saw the thoughts churning behind Zane's little eyes.

"He ain't gonna shoot us," Zane said. "He can't. He knows Ma might hear the shots." The man's fat face broke into an evil smile. "Let's get him," he rasped, and lunged forward, Zeb joining in a few paces behind.

Fargo's oath remained inside as he brought his body into a half-crouch, waiting for the two fat forms to charge directly at him. When Zane had his outstretched hands only inches from him, Fargo swerved, spun to one side, and the man charged past. Still in the half-crouch, Fargo brought the barrel of the Colt up in an arc. It smashed into Zane's temple as the man halted and started to turn. The paunchy figure staggered back, a line of red coursing down the side of his face.

Fargo started to bring up a long, looping left hook when he saw Zeb charging from the side. Again he twisted away, then stuck out one leg and sent Zeb sprawling. The man was still on his hands and knees when Fargo brought the barrel of the Colt down on the back of his head. The fat hulk fell facedown and lay quivering on the ground.

But Zane was lunging again and Fargo realized there was no time to turn and meet the charge. He threw himself forward in a headlong dive, but the big man's body slammed into the bottom of his legs. Fargo was knocked sideways, and he brought his arms in as he hit the ground. His finger started to tighten, an automatic reaction, but he managed to restrain it before the gun went off. He rolled, came up on his feet, and realized the split-second mistake could easily happen again, a shot exploding before he could stop it. He flung the Colt aside and saw Zane's small eyes light up as the man came at him again.

Zane was in charge this time, circling, his fists upraised. Fargo saw the fat hulk on the ground lift itself up, pause on hands and knees, and rise to its feet. No sense, no feeling, he swore silently.

Zane tried a roundhouse right that Fargo parried with ease and dug an answering hard left into the man's paunch. Zane took a half-step backward and sucked in air, but the blubber was a ring of protection. He came forward again. Fargo swung, a sharp left hook that landed on the man's jaw, and again Zane took a step backward. He blinked and came forward again. This time the folds of fat around his neck had helped absorb the effect of the blow and he plodded forward again.

"Get behind him, Zeb," Zane called out, and Fargo flicked a glance to the side to see Zeb start to circle behind him. He feinted to his left but Zane moved with more quickness than he'd expected.

Fargo cast a glance over his shoulder and saw Zeb closing in. In front of him, head lowered, arms upraised, Zane started toward him again. "Get him," Zane rasped, and lunged forward.

Fargo had no need to turn to know Zeb charged also, the man's heavy pounding steps shaking the ground. The Trailsman stayed, every muscle tensed, waited another split second as Zane's hands reached for his throat. With one, quick motion, he dropped, twisted, threw himself flat on the ground, and he heard the thudding sound as Zane and Zeb slammed into each other; the sharp crack of their meeting skulls was exactly the sound he wanted to hear.

Fargo scrambled forward, leapt to his feet. Zane and Zeb's paunchy forms still faced each other as they staggered back, each one with a stream of red coming down his forehead. Fargo swung, all his strength behind the blow, a looping right that landed on Zane's jaw and, but a half-second later, spun and smashed a looping left into Zeb's jaw. Both men staggered again, both fell on one knee. Fargo chose Zane first, brought a roundhouse right that smashed full into the man's face and Zane fell backward with a crashing thud. The Trailsman spun again and smashed a left into Zeb's face and the man staggered back, then collapsed onto the ground not unlike a giant balloon that had lost air but somehow remained largely inflated.

Fargo drew back, then glanced across at Ted and Tim. The two boys raced to his side, throwing their arms around him. He smiled and saw the fear in their faces begin to slide away. "You can help me tie them up," he said as he crouched down and put his arms around both boys. He drew back and saw the sudden horror fill Tim's eyes.

"Fargo!" Tim screamed, and fell away. Fargo turned

to see the hulking figure, blood streaking down its face, half-fall, half-lunge at him. Through the streams of blood he managed to see it was Zane, and he tried to twist aside but the man was too close. His full weight slammed over him and Fargo went down. He managed to turn his face aside and the man's blood spattered past him, but Zane's hands had found his throat, and his weight made Fargo almost immobile. But he could move his arms, so he brought his hands up and tried to tear the man's fingers from around his throat. But the meaty hands were locked around his throat and he fought out of raging fury. Like a wounded buffalo, the dullard's level of sensitivity made him insensate to the pain and wounds that would stop ordinary creatures. Fargo felt the breath gushing from him. He brought his arm down and managed to lift his leg enough to reach the double-edged throwing knife in the calf holster. He yanked the blade free and felt the last of his breath rasp in his throat. He brought the blade up and plunged it into Zane's arm first, and with a guttural sound the man pulled his arm back. As air rushed into his lungs, Fargo struck again with the slender blade, driving into the side of Zane's neck.

Zane's lips parted as he half-fell, half-turned away, and Fargo pulled himself free of the oppressive weight. A new stream of blood gushed from Zane's neck as he fell onto his back, rolled, and made futile motions in the air.

But Fargo spun, on one knee, in time to see Zeb coming at him, almost a bloodied carbon copy of his brother. Fargo drew his arm back and sent the throwing knife hurtling through the air. The blade slammed into the man just below his collarbone, plunged in all the way to the hilt, and quivered there as Zeb tottered, took a last step forward, and fell, his body hitting the ground with a large and lifeless thud. Fargo waited a moment before he stepped to the man and pulled the knife free. He wiped the blade clean and returned it to the calf holster. The boys stared transfixed at the two still mounds of flesh. He went over to them and gently turned them away.

"Didn't plan for it to end this way," Fargo said. "But they forced it. Then, they had two strikes against them." Both boys looked at him with their eyes questioning. "Being no good was one. Being stupid was the other," Fargo finished, and steered them to the horses.

He had Tim ride one and took the other with Ted. When they reached the place where he'd left the Ovaro he changed mounts and left each boy with a horse. When they neared the camp, he motioned for the boys to be quiet and had them dismount in the center of the strip of land.

He climbed onto Ma Cowley's wagon and stepped inside. Cassie sat up at once atop a narrow mattress in one corner and Fargo waited for an instant as Ma Cowley snapped awake. She sat up, a voluminous nightdress surrounding her massive breasts.

"What the hell are you doing here?" she roared, and reached for the rifle. Fargo's hand shot out and knocked the gun away. He brought his arm around the side of her head, took hold of a handful of the long, matted hair, and yanked the woman to her feet.

"Ow," she yelled as he propelled her to the opening flap of the canvas.

"Outside," he said, pushed her head through, drew back his leg, and put one foot against the mountainous rump. He shoved hard and the huge woman went tumbling out of the wagon with a scream and a curse. Fargo followed her out as she lay on the ground, nightdress billowing while she pushed herself to her feet.

"Goddammit," the woman swore, and halted, froze in place as she focused on the two boys. She stared at them, her jaw dropping open.

"You're not seeing things," Fargo said, and swung down from the wagon.

Ma Cowley turned to him, her eyes glowing with

venemous apprehension. "Zeb and Zane," she muttered, and Fargo made no reply. The apprehension became pure hatred in the woman's small eyes.

"You son of a bitch. You shit bastard son of a bitch," the huge woman snarled.

"You made them and you used them," Fargo returned coldly. "They paid your dues."

"I'll kill you, Fargo," Ma Cowley snarled.

Fargo met the hatred she flung at him. But the noise had brought the camp awake. Vera leapt out of the Conestoga and gathered Ted and Tim into her arms; Cassie, the wool jacket on, came out of the wagon, and Gabe Hazzard moved toward her.

"Tie her up," Fargo said. He motioned to Ma Cowley. "I'll do you myself," he said.

"Let me put a dress on first," the woman protested.

"Go on," Fargo said, and followed Ma Cowley as she climbed into the wagon.

The woman turned and glared at him. "Get out of here," she barked.

"And give you a chance to pull something off? Forget it," Fargo said.

"I'm not changing with you here," the woman insisted.

"I promise not to get too excited," Fargo said. "Change or I'll tie you up like that. Make up your damn mind."

"Bastard," the woman said, turned away, and pulled the nightdress over her head.

Fargo smiled as he saw the imprint of his foot still red on the fleshy mountain of her rump. She reached for the black, one-piece tentlike dress, and Fargo glimpsed the massive breasts swaying from side to side as she moved, brownish tips that might have been huge on an ordinary woman but seemed tiny on her. She drew the garment on over her head and her fleshy folds disappeared under the dress.

Fargo backed from the wagon and saw Gabe Hazzard waiting with the rope in his hands. When the woman emerged and swung to the ground, Fargo helped tie her arms to her sides and her wrists together. With Gabe Hazzard, he helped boost her back into the wagon and put Cassie inside with her.

He turned to the others still gathered in the darkness, Vera cradling the boys against her. "One man outside this wagon at all times, two-hour shifts," he said to Gabe Hazzard, and the foreman nodded. "Now I'm going to get some sleep. We'll talk, come morning," Fargo said, and strode away.

The others drifted to their wagons and blankets, and Fargo settled down against the rocks where he'd left his bedroll. The deep sigh that came from his lips echoed the weariness inside him. The night wind held its bite and he slept, but not nearly as soundly as he wanted.

7

When the gray morning came he had Ma Cowley and Cassie untied, but only long enough for them to have coffee and porridge. When the meal was finished he had them tied and put against their wagon as he faced the others. Before he spoke he swept the high crags with a long glance and let the others follow his eyes as they paused at the line of Nez Percé outlined against the morning sky.

"Only six," he said. "But you can be damn sure there are twenty more waiting nearby." Fargo scanned the knot of figures that waited in front of him.

Harriet clung to Abel Gunnard's arm; Gabe Hazzard and the remainder of his crew stood in a cluster of their own. He saw Hope with Ted and Tim beside her.

"Where's Vera?" Fargo asked.

"Inside the wagon. She's real sick, been throwing up all night. Everything's gotten to her, I guess," Hope said.

Fargo nodded, his eyes grim as he scanned the others. "You all pretty well know what I'm going to say, but I'll spell it out for you once more," he began. "We've only gotten this far because Walking Deer gave me his promise he'd wait. We're only a few hours from the top of Blood Pass. If we go on, we're only one hour away from being massacred." He paused and saw Gabe Hazzard shift uncomfortably. "I'm going back. I'll take whoever wants to come with me."

"Count us in," Gabe Hazzard said, obviously talking for the rest of his crew, and Fargo saw the pain in Abel Gunnard's glance at the man. The foreman returned an apologetic shrug. "Sorry, Abel, but Fargo's been right all along. It's pretty damn plain that he's right now, and none of us hanker to be massacred. There's no point in going on any farther."

Fargo directed his gaze at Abel Gunnard and it was Harriet who answered as Gunnard stared at the ground. "We'll be going back with you," she said softly.

Fargo nodded and turned to Hope.

"Guess there's nothing else left to do," she said. "But Vera's too sick to travel today. She's running a fever, too. All from her upset, I'd guess. But she needs a full day of rest before starting back. Can't we wait till tomorrow morning?"

Fargo's eyes went to the waiting bronzed figures on their sturdy ponies. "Everybody stays right here in the camp. Nobody sets one foot outside," he said. "One day only. They won't wait more than that. I just hope they'll give us another day."

"Why not if we're just staying here?" Harriet asked.

"We've interrupted their winter preparations. They can't let us keep them from that any longer than we have," Fargo said, and his eyes went to Hope. "We move out, come morning, sick or not."

"What about us?" Ma Cowley snapped with unwarranted authority.

"I'm taking you back with us, unless you give me any trouble," Fargo said. There was no need to explain the unstated. "Take the time to check the wagons, go over your tack," he said, and cast an eye at the gray sky above. "And if you've a mind to, you can pray," he added.

They turned away in silence and went about their own business while he moved to the Ovaro and unsaddled the horse. Using a sweat scraper and a dandy brush, he took his time and gave his horse a good grooming, pausing to cast a glance at Ma Cowley and Cassie from time to time. Both the huge woman and the slender girl stayed seated against the wagon until the dusk began to come down from the high crags. The six Nez Percé warriors were still in place, still watching, and Abe Jones made a meager supper for everyone.

"We can find some more grouse when we get down into the middle range," Fargo said. He saw that Abel Gunnard didn't eat anything, his face a somber mask as he stared into space. When the meal ended, Gunnard crept into his wagon while Harriet stayed outside a few moments longer. "Going back won't be a lark," Fargo said. "He'd best pull himself together."

"Losing a dream hurts," Harriet said.

"Losing your scalp hurts more," Fargo muttered, and walked on to where Gabe Hazzard rested. "I want everybody fresh and fit for hard riding tomorrow." Fargo pointed to Ma Cowley and Cassie. "Tie them into the wagon for the night. Then we won't need somebody watching them."

The foreman nodded agreement and Fargo took his bedroll to the side of the narrow strip of land again. He set his things out and grimaced at the dampness of the night air. He waited for the camp to quiet down before he settled in himself and lay quietly, letting his thoughts idle. He knew he'd count himself lucky if they were past the middle range when the snows came. They were coming, he was certain of that. The signs rode the night wind, the warnings painted in the gray skies and the hard ground. It was not over, Fargo told himself as uneasiness gnawed at him. He closed his eyes, tried to sleep and found the surcease of slumber hung out of reach. Finally, no longer able to ignore the misgivings that continued to stab at him, he dressed and stepped to the edge of the camp, let his eyes slowly scan the darkness.

Fargo moved toward the high-sided farm wagon, pulled himself up onto the front end, and pulled the canvas flap aside. It took a moment for his eyes to adjust to the darkness. Ma Cowley's mountainous form was easy enough to see, but he struggled to peer into the shadows of the far corner of the wagon, finally spotting Cassie on the mattress, hands and feet bound together.

He backed out and dropped to the ground and the disquiet still stayed with him. He scanned the camp again, his gaze slowly moving over the sleeping forms of Gabe Hazzard and his men, past Abel Gunnard's wagon and the horses tethered near it. He started to move on, then froze and stared straight ahead. One of the horses was missing. He stepped closer, counted again, he'd made no mistake. In three swift strides he was at the Conestoga, leaping onto the wagon and pulling the canvas back.

The boys were asleep in one corner but Vera looked up at once with her haunted eyes. There was no one else in the wagon.

"She's gone, hasn't she?" he hissed. Vera nodded. "Goddammit, how could you let her?" Fargo swore.

"I was going to go," Vera said. "We're so close. I couldn't turn back without knowing. I had to go, to try to find out."

"Only she wouldn't let you," Fargo bit out, and Vera nodded again, embracing herself with both arms.

"She said I had to stay with the boys," Vera murmured. "She made me promise to stay if she went in my place. I asked her to let me go, but she refused and finally I agreed."

"When?" Fargo asked. "Last night?" He swore again as Vera nodded. "You weren't sick all day. She used that to keep me here overnight so she could pull this off."

The woman nodded again and met his fury with her wan, drawn face. "We're so close. I have to know," she intoned, and kept her arms wrapped around herself.

"Fools, all of you. Stupid fools," Fargo shot back. "How long ago did she leave?"

"An hour ago, maybe a little more," Vera answered.

Fargo whirled and leapt from the wagon. He saw Gabe Hazzard sit up as he hit the ground. "If I'm not here by morning, you start back," Fargo said.

"What's going on?" Gabe Hazzard asked.

"No time to explain now. You just take the way we came, understand?" Fargo answered.

"I'll do my best," the man said as Fargo strode to the Ovaro, threw the saddle on the horse, and pulled the cinch tight.

"I'll be catching up to you, I hope," Fargo said, pulling himself onto the horse.

"If you don't?" Hazzard asked.

"Good luck," Fargo grunted, and sent the pinto into a fast trot. He swung onto the pass and rode north, dreading the task ahead. Hope must have walked the horse from the camp. He would have heard her otherwise. She had been very clever, but she had also had a slow start. He kept the pinto going at a fast trot, unwilling to risk the pounding echo of a gallop, but there was no need to halt and find her tracks. She was moving toward one goal, and he hoped she continued being clever and careful. Otherwise, all he'd find would be her arrow-riddled body.

He looked up, made a note of the dim pale sphere barely visible behind the clouds, and returned his eyes to the narrow ribbon that was Blood Pass. He fought away the urge to increase his pace and held the pinto back as the horse fought to race through the dark, cold night, anxious to run free. As he rode, Fargo continued to glance up at the sky where only a pale gray-white circle marked the moon's progress. But the circle had moved, marking time and distance with its own accuracy. The path began to level off.

Fargo pulled the Ovaro to a slow trot and then to a walk. He took the calculated risk of moving on a few hundred more yards, then halted. He swung to the ground and led the Ovaro into the northern spruce at the side of the pass. He tied the horse out of sight in the trees and returned to the pass, dropped to one knee, and peered at the soil. He ran his fingers across the earth and grimaced. She was still riding when she'd reached here, but she had perhaps another fifty yards' cushion. If she didn't dismount by then, she was headed for certain death.

But she wasn't more than another hundred yards or so ahead, he estimated, and he rose and broke into the long, loping stride that let him move as silently as a wolf. He moved forward and halted again after another twenty yards, dropped down to peer at the ground and run his fingers across it again. He nodded as he rose, a grim admiration inside him. She left the horse, hid the animal somewhere, as he had the Ovaro, and was moving cautiously on foot.

Fargo went into the loping stride again, moved to the side of the path, and strained to peer through the night. Suddenly he spied her, moving ahead carefully, aware of her nearness to the top of the pass. Fargo looked past the dark shadow of Hope's figure as he moved closer to her. He frowned as his wild-creature vision picked out the tall, thin shapes that rose from the ground. The first scaffold of the sacred burial ground was close, too close, he swore silently, swerved, and dug his heels into the hard earth.

Hope had slowed, moved cautiously, all her concentration on the path ahead. She never heard Fargo as he dived, brought one hand around to clap it over her mouth, and hit the ground half atop her. He held her there, using his weight to keep her motionless.

"Shut up," he hissed. "It's me." He felt her body relax, so he drew his hand from her mouth and pushed away. She rolled to face him, her eyes still round with astonishment. She wore a black cape over a black shirt, with a dark skirt. His eyes were filled with bitter fury as she pushed herself up to a sitting position. "Fool. Goddamn fool," he rasped.

"I had to or Vera would've gone," she said.

"I heard," Fargo interrupted. "You're both fools. And you're going back."

"No," she said. "Not when I'm this close."

"You're this close to being dead," Fargo said. "Their burial ground guards are there. You can't see them from here."

"I'll get by them. I'll find a way," she said.

"You're going back if I have to knock you out and carry you," Fargo hissed.

She started to protest again when the sound came

through the night, the soft thud of unshod Indian ponies.

Fargo threw himself forward and pushed Hope to the ground, his hand over her mouth. Her eyes filled with alarm at once as she heard the sound and looked at him over the edge of his hand. "Quiet," he breathed fiercely. She nodded. He drew his hand back. He turned his head, saw the four ponies and their riders moving up the pass. They came to a halt a dozen yards back, and the four braves slid to the ground.

"Are they looking for us?" Hope whispered.

"No," Fargo said, watching the Indians settle down on both sides of the pass. "They're setting up for the morning, in case the wagons try to rush through and the other warriors don't stop them in time. But they've cut us off, goddammit," Fargo swore, his voice a harsh whisper. He swore again, under his breath this time. They were trapped with only one way to go—forward.

He glanced at the land on both sides of the pass. It was sheer rock, too smooth and too high to climb. "Hell," he murmured. "Dammit to hell." Their only chance was to cross the sacred burial ground to the other side. He swore again, for it was a devil's choice, but there was no other. "We'll have to try to get across to the other side of the pass. We stay here and they'll see us with the first light," he whispered. "On your belly." Hope frowned at him. "We leave footprints and we might just as well announce that we've been here," he said. "Stay with me." He went down onto his stomach and began to crawl, inching his way along the ground.

Hope stayed close to him, rested when he did, and moved forward again with him. The few dozen yards to the edge of the burial ground seemed a mile, but finally Fargo halted in front of the first tall scaffold, raised his head carefully, and peered along the ground to the far right. He searched along the edge of the burial grounds and finally spied the two silent figures leaning against a flat rock, a lance beside each one. He turned his head, peered down the other side, and saw two more Nez Percé sentries. From both ends of the burial grounds, they could see the approach of the pass from either side. By day it would have been impossible to draw near even by crawling, but the darkness was a lifesaving ally. Now Fargo's eyes peered through the maze of silent poles. They were a grim forest, each supporting a palette on which a still figure lay, some newly wrapped in burial shrouds, others in tattered sheets. Still others were merely bare bones that rattled against one another in the night wind. That wind whistled softly through this forest of death; it seemed that the great spirits wailed and that this was indeed a sacred ground.

"Crawl," Fargo whispered.

"No, I can't, not through the very center," Hope murmured.

He brought one hand up and closed it around the back of her neck. "There's no other way. You had to come. Now you're here, dammit. Crawl," he hissed, and began to inch forward again.

She moved, staying against him as she did. He crawled under the first high palette, flattened against the ground as the wind softly wailed and sobbed through the scaffoldings. Inching his way forward, keeping his head down, he made painfully slow progress, but finally reached the center of the burial grounds and halted. He felt Hope trembling as she lay against him. In that instant he almost felt sorry for her. This was a place of forces that were more than imaginings. He felt it, too, the presence of more than is given us to understand. Maybe the red man's beliefs were fashioned of superstition and myths, but on that sacred ground, the cathedral made of wood and wind, there were forces beyond ordinary understanding.

Fargo reached out, put a hand against Hope's face, a silent message, and began to inch forward again. She crawled beside him as he continued the agonizingly slow progress. With the wailing of the wind there was a strange silence that had its own chilling effect, and Fargo felt an intangible tension inside himself. When the last scaffold rose up over him, Fargo felt the relief grab him, but he shot a harsh glance at Hope and motioned for her to continue to crawl with her head down. She stayed alongside him as he snaked his way along the other side of Blood Pass, the road slanting downward almost at once.

The moon had disappeared entirely. Daybreak was near, but he forced himself to stay flattened on the ground. It wasn't until he'd gone another hundred yards that he rose and rested on one knee. Hope pushed herself up beside him, cape undone, breasts pushing against the black blouse with every deep breath she drew in. The first grayness of the new day came to the sky and she met the icy stare he turned on her.

"I didn't know it'd be like this," she said.

"You didn't know and you didn't care," Fargo rasped. "Stubborn and stupid."

"I couldn't let Vera go," she murmured.

"You could've called me," Fargo snapped. "You wanted to find out for her and for yourself. You can't keep pointing at her."

She looked away at the harsh truth he flung at her, pushed to her feet, and straightened up. "I'm going on. I'm going to find that lean-to. Maybe that'll tell me something," she said.

He made no reply and fell in step beside her as she went on. "We have until tonight. Then we go back." He saw the dismay leap into her round, brown eyes. "There's no other way. Maybe we'll be lucky twice," he said.

"Are the others waiting for us?" she queried.

"They've started back by now," he said. "The Nez Percé will watch, stay with them for a day, and then let them go on alone. Unless . . . ."

"Unless what?" Hope frowned.

"Unless something happens to let them know the sacred burial ground has been violated," he said.

"Like seeing us," she added.

"That would sure as hell do it. So would finding my horse. Or yours," Fargo said. "That'd be enough to

140

let them put the rest together. They'll come raging then, out to kill everyone and anyone."

Hope stayed quiet as she took in his words. It was another five minutes when she turned to him. "You must hate me," she said. "You wouldn't be here if it weren't for me."

"Let's say I'm not too damn happy with you," he growled.

She halted abruptly and turned to him. Her arms slid around his neck, a quick, almost desperate motion, and he felt the softness of her lips as she pressed her mouth to his. Her kiss held, warm and pressing. His mouth opened and responded as she stayed a moment longer, then pulled back. Her brown eyes sought his with sincerity. "I'm sorry," she said. "For getting you into this. I wanted to do it all by myself. You shouldn't have followed me."

"You sorry about that, too?" he asked.

"No. I'd never have made it alone. But not being sorry about that is just selfish. I wish we were someplace else and sometime else, just the two of us. That honest enough for you?" she asked.

"Better late than never," he said. "But we're not, so let's keep going." She nodded, and this time, as she walked, he found her hand in his, her fingers clasped tightly around his. He glanced up at the gray sky and swore, his eyes drawn to the terrain that bordered the pass. There was more rock, more steep hills, and he spotted at least two caves as they walked on. He was still scanning the surrounding hills when Hope's hand tightened around his, and he instantly peered forward to see the small, sagging structure built along one edge of the pass.

"It's the lean-to," Hope said, and began to run. "You see, his letter was all true. He made it." She ran and Fargo followed, reaching the small lean-to as she did. He saw the hole in the roof, the two walls sagging. The stones of a fireplace were still in place and there were two rooms, a larger one opening out in the front, and another set behind it.

Fargo halted beside Hope and swept the first room with a quick glance. He saw animal droppings, a broken chair, small ridges of dust that had collected for months. The shelter had plainly not been lived in for a while, as long as a year, he guessed. He stepped to the doorway of the other room and halted, his lips thinning. What had once been a mattress, now but the remains of torn and ripped material, lay in one corner. On top of it, a skeleton stretched out, bone arms upraised with four arrows protruding between the bones of what had once been a flesh-and-muscle chest.

He turned as Hope came forward and uttered a short gasped cry as she stared down at the arrow-riddled skeleton. She spun and ran from the lean-to. Fargo followed her outside where she stood with her fists clenched. "It could've been anybody, a trapper who'd used the lean-to," she bit out.

Fargo nodded and returned to the back room. He stepped closer to the skeleton and carefully examined the torn and shredded remains of the mattress and the floor beside it. He halted beside the wooden box that had apparently served as an end table beside the bed. He picked up the thin, gold chain, a small heart-shaped pendant hanging from it, and walked outside to where Hope's eyes still held the refusal to accept what she'd seen.

He waited until he reached her before opening his hand. She looked down at the chin and pendant. Her cry was a half-sob of anguish and defeat, and she fell against him, her face buried into his chest. "Vera gave him that before they were married," she murmured. "Oh, God. Oh, my God."

"You wanted an answer," he said, and tried to soften the harshness in his voice. "Yes, he got through, somehow, but they found out," Fargo said. "They found out, followed him here, and made him pay for it." He held her as he put the rest together in his mind. Her brother had managed to crawl through, probably much as they had, but he'd felt too confident then. He'd left footprints and the Nez Percé had read them correctly. The rest was foreordained.

Fargo lifted his head to peer into the rock hills alongside the pass. Hope went with him in silence as he left the pass and began to climb along the edge of the hills. He turned sharply and pulled his way up a narrow crevice, stayed with it until he spotted a small opening in one of the rock hillsides. He bent low to enter the cave and found that it broadened enough for him to stand up. It smelled less dank and musty than most caves and seemed free of animal odor, probably due to the high crag terrain beyond the territory of most creatures. A slight breeze wafted from the back; there was probably a small opening at the rear. The draft made it cold and he saw Hope shiver.

"Do we have to stay here?" she asked.

"We've got to stay out of sight till night. Roaming around could mean being spotted," he said. He glanced around at the cave again. A small fire would warm it in minutes, and it was deep enough, the ceiling high enough, for smoke to dissipate before the breeze would carry it out into the air. It was also deep enough in the high crags to be out of the way.

"Settle in. I'll be right back," he said, and hurried outside. He gathered an armful of dry branches and returned with them. He went back and brought in another armful. "We'll be here till dark," he said, and to be extra careful, he found enough loose rocks to pile in front of the entrance so the smoke that left would become only wispy trails after moving through and over the rocks, trails that the wind would erase immediately. Satisfied with what he'd done, he got the fire going. The light showed the cave to be relatively clean with a bed of soft moss growing over the stones at one side.

The fire warmed the small area even more quickly than he'd imagined it would. Hope took the cape off, spread it out over the moss, and lay down on it.

Fargo watched her and smiled. She sat up quickly.

"That attack of honesty was short, wasn't it?" he answered.

"Here?" She frowned.

"It's someplace else and sometime else," Fargo said, reminded her. "And we've most of the day to wait."

Her eyes held his, round and warm. The tiny smile touched the corners of her lips. "You think it was just talk, a moment of recklessness," she said. "Not real honesty."

"Wouldn't surprise me," he admitted.

She rose to her feet and her hand went to the neck of the black blouse. Slowly, she began to unbutton it. He watched and waited, but she didn't stop. When the last button was undone, she let the blouse fall away and stood before him, her breasts full and round, each tipped with a pink point set in a small circle of matching pink. Her shoulders echoed the lovely breasts, soft and very rounded and broad. "Does this surprise you?" she asked.

"That you're so damn good-looking? No, that doesn't surprise me," Fargo said.

"That I'd do this," she corrected with some impatience.

"Damn few things women do surprise me, honey," Fargo said. "I figure you've good reason. I only hope it's being hungry more than grateful."

"It is," she said. "More honesty."

"Good. It'll be turned around when we're through," Fargo said, and she frowned.

"Turned around?"

"You'll be more grateful than hungry," he said, and cupped his hands around her two lovely breasts. She gasped, a short, breathy sound. He helped her as she flipped the hook of the skirt and the garment tumbled to the ground followed by the pair of pink bloomers. He took in generous hips, a very black, curly nap that narrowed down to smooth-fleshed thighs that just avoided heaviness. Hope Maxwell had a rounded body, everything well-covered, everything echoing itself. He shed clothes as she watched him, suddenly holding herself very still until he closed his arms around her, pulled her soft, warm body to him. She cried out at the touch of him, the feel of his pulsating maleness pressed against her rounded belly.

He lay down with her on the cape, and her mouth opened for his, her kisses soft yet hard, sweet yet burning. When he brought his lips down to the very round, soft breasts, her body twisted, hips moving to one side then the other. She called out, a half-groan, half-cry. "Aaaagggh . . . oh, God . . . aaaaagh," she breathed, and her hands clasped his head, held his face against her round, full breasts as he caressed each pink tip with his tongue, pulled gently with his lips. Again Hope screamed in delight. He let his hand steal down across her abdomen, press into the softly rounded belly, and probe the black curliness, and she cried out in a steady stream of tiny gasps. His mouth still closed around one full round breast when his hand slid down to cup the dark moistness of her and Hope's pelvis lifted, quivered, and sank down again. The tiny sounds came from her, wordless tributes to pleasure. He held his hand against her, let it grow warm with the wet heat of her, and she cried out, her fingers sliding down to press against his hand. "Inside, Fargo . . . inside, please," she whispered, and her fleshy thighs fell open, the offering of offerings, the gift unlike any other.

He moved, obeyed, let his fingers probe gently and caress the soft inner lips. Hope cried out and her pelvis writhed, turned, twisted, and her moans grew more fervid as he probed deeper. "Yes, yes . . . aaaaaah, yes," Hope breathed, each word, each sound a long, almost endless hiss. When he turned and brought himself over her, she half-screamed in the anticipation of ecstasy. Her thighs opened then closed around him, and her hands reached down to clasp at his buttocks as she half-lifted herself upward. "Take me, oh, please, please take me," she called out, and pulled him to her. He felt the surging desire inside himself spill out as he plunged into her. She screamed in pure pleasure as he filled her, sweet friction of throbbing flesh against quivering flesh.

The round, full breasts seemed to bounce as Hope pushed with him, matched his every sliding thrust with her own movements. She stayed with him longer than he'd expected, seeking to gather in every last second of ecstasy. Her fleshy thighs opened, then came hard against him with a sudden surge of fervor, and he heard the urgency fill her gasped sounds. Her hands squeezed hard against his shoulders, moved up to his neck, and pulled his face down into the round, full breasts. "Now, oh, yes, now, it's now, now . . . aaaiiiii," Hope sang out, her voice a rising crescendo of rapture. He let his own spiral of sensation explode with a wondrously sweet union, all the senses coming together. As two streams joining, they flowed together, the world a moment made still.

"Oh, God," Hope breathed as she sank back, though he stayed inside her. He started to pull his mouth back from her breast but she clutched him against her. "No, stay . . . stay," she murmured, and he did, warming the round loveliness with the heat of his mouth. Finally he slid from her, and as the soft sphere pulled from his lips, she pushed her body against his, turning to lie half atop him. Her brown eyes studied his chiseled handsomeness. "Maybe you weren't surprised, but I was," she said. "It all seemed so important so suddenly."

"The mind holds its own notions," he said. "It makes us listen to what's under our thoughts."

"Like being afraid of never having another chance," Hope said, and pushed up on one elbow to look down at him. "But you were wrong about one thing," she said, and his eyes questioned. "I'm still more hungry than grateful."

"It's not over. We've a good spell of time left." Fargo grinned.

Her round eyes took on a twinkle. "That's nice," she murmured, and brought her lips down upon his mouth. Her hands caressed his face, moved down along his shoulders, and gently traced a path down the muscled beauty of his chest.

He felt himself gathering renewed strength and desire, quick to rekindle itself as Hope slid down along his body and her lips moved across his skin, a slow path punctuated by tiny nibbles as she reached his flat abdomen. She continued to move slowly down his body, rubbed the round, full breasts against him until she came to the hotly pulsating gift. He groaned with pleasure at the touch of her lips, warm, sweet, caressing. Hope made tiny pleasure sounds as she caressed, explored, fondled, and her delight became desire as she emitted low, groaning sounds. She grasped him as she brought her fleshy thighs up, pushed the curly black triangle forward, and enveloped him, shuddering satisfaction in the long sigh she uttered.

He made love with her more slowly this time, and her cries of passion and pleasure curled through the cave, echoed back on one another until the small space reverberated with her sighs and gasped delights. Her rounded body twisted and pushed, rose and fell with his lovemaking, and her arms clasped and unclasped around him, hands pulling at him, then pushing, grasping and caressing. There was no part of her unbathed in the fine dew of perspiration when she finally cried out in climax. She gasped out long harsh breaths when she lay still beside the small fire. Fargo enjoyed the beauty of her rounded curves, the soft smoothness of her, the fleshy thighs that were still firm and sensually lovely.

He lay beside her, closed his eyes with her, and enjoyed the half-sleep of satiation until he stirred and sat up. He started to draw on clothes and Hope woke, round eyes growing fearful at once. He nodded at the unasked question in their brown depths. The fire had almost died out and the cold quickly began to take command of the little cave again. He pulled her to her feet and, when she was dressed, drew the black cape around her. "Crawling back through the burial grounds won't be any easier," he warned her, and she nodded, her face set. "You stay beside me, just the way you did before," he said.

"Don't worry about that," she said grimly.

"They'll have taken away that roadblock on the other side of the pass," Fargo said. "If we can get through the burial grounds, we can get to the horses and be on our way." He stamped out the last of the embers and the cave was plunged into blackness, but her hand found his and she followed as he moved toward the entranceway. He halted there, carefully moved aside the pyramid of rocks, then stepped into the night and cursed. A thin mantle of white covered the ground and a few flakes still drifted down from the dark sky.

8

"It's not snowing heavily. It's certainly no blizzard," Hope said with a frown. "It won't bother me any."

"But it'll leave the marks of where we crawled, and footprints afterward," Fargo bit out. "And there's no way to avoid it, goddammit," he swore.

"We'll be on our way before they find the tracks," Hope said. "Maybe even caught up to the others."

"You still don't understand, do you? They'll come after us. The sacred ground has been defiled. Only destroying those who did it will satisfy the gods," Fargo bit out. He threw a bitter glance up at the sky. Mother Nature had conspired to answer the defiance of her power. Or had the Nez Percé spirit gods invoked their strengths? No burying blizzard of howling white. Death administered by a rapier instead of a sledgehammer. But the price was the same. He could almost hear the sound of mocking laughter in the wind as he gazed down at the thin mantle of white. With a curse curled inside him, he started forward with Hope at his side.

He moved quickly along the pass, no reason for stepping carefully now. Only when he came in sight of the forest of scaffolding and palettes did he stop and drop to one knee. "You start crawling here," he said. "Inch by inch."

"Where are you going?" she asked, fear instant in her eyes.

"To buy us a few more hours, I hope. If we get through, they'll see our marks in the snow, come dawn. They'll race down to tell the others. If I can get rid of the sentries, it'll be at least three or four hours before someone finds them, maybe longer. We'll need every bit of that time." He rose to a crouch when he finished, and darted to the edge of the pass. Staying in the rocks that lined the pass, he moved forward, clambered over some, found his way through crevices in others, and halted when he reached the edge of the burial grounds. He searched the darkness and found the nearest sentry standing against the high, flat rock.

The man leaned on the stone but he was very much awake, peering across the trees of scaffolding in front of him. Fargo dropped low and drew the double-edged, pencil-thin throwing knife from its calf holster. He moved closer, still edging along the side rocks until they came to an end. There was only the last high stone with the sentry standing against it and, beyond that, the forest of scaffolds. He crept a half-dozen steps closer and suddenly the Indian straightened, peered forward, and took a tighter grip on the lance he carried in one hand. But Fargo's arm was upraised, his eyes measuring distance, trajectory, angle. He sent the blade hurtling through the air with all the strength in his powerful arm and shoulder muscles, watched it fly through the night, and was racing forward even before it landed, long legs digging his feet into the ground. The knife slammed into the guard just as the man half-turned, suddenly aware of the weapon hurtling at him. It hit going downward, plunged through his jawbone and into his neck. He staggered, then stood very still for a moment. Fargo was at him as he started to topple over, the lance falling from his hand. Fargo grabbed the lance before it hit the ground, managed to get his other arm out and slow the Indian's fall so he didn't hit the ground with a full thud.

On one knee beside the Indian, Fargo yanked his blade free, wiped it clean, and turned, the lance in one hand. The shout came from the other side of the burial grounds. He had not worked silently enough, and he stayed on one knee as the second guard called out again. Without an answer, the man would go into action immediately, and Fargo knew he dared not use his gun. The night stillness and the echoing crags would send the sound too far. He remained on one knee and brought the lance to his right hand as he peered through the scaffolds. The second guard was moving toward him, he was certain, carefully threading his way across the burial grounds, aware that something was wrong. Fargo edged a step backward to the deepest shadows beside the rock and peered through the darkness.

The thin mantle of snow silhouetted the tall sparse scaffolds where they rose from the ground. Fargo's eyes darted back and forth across the width of the sacred ground until suddenly he spotted the figure moving in a crouch. The Indian also carried a lance in one hand as he moved on careful, silent steps, brushing past one of the tall scaffolds, moving closer. Fargo knew the Nez Percé was still too far away to see clearly, so he stayed motionless. The Indian had reached the center of the burial grounds when Fargo almost cursed aloud as he spotted the black, flattened form inching along the ground, almost at the front edge of the first row of burial palettes. She'd been hurrying, dammit, Fargo swore, crawling too fast. She ought to still be a dozen yards away.

But she wasn't and he cursed again silently as he saw the Indian suddenly halt, his head turn as he picked up the flat, unformed shape against the snow. Fargo saw the Nez Percé shift his direction and start toward Hope, who, crawling with her head down was totally unaware of the figure moving toward her. Fargo broke from the shadows, moving on the balls of his feet, grateful for the cushioning silence of the new snow. He saw the Nez Percé halt, growing aware that the strange shape was someone crawling across the sacred ground. The Indian took six quick steps forward with catlike movement and Fargo saw him bring the lance up.

Hope, instincts surging at her, lifted her head in time to see the Indian coming at her, the lance raised to plunge into her body. Her scream shattered the

night and covered the sound of Fargo's pounding footsteps as he raced between the silent palettes overhead.
Not daring to waste another split second, he flung the
lance just as the Nez Percé started to plunge his downward. Fargo's weapon struck with full force into the
Indian's back, and the man gave a guttural cry of pain,
staggering forward as he brought his own lance downward. But his blow overshot his target by six inches as
he staggered, and Fargo saw the lance plunge into the
edge of Hope's cape. Pinned in place, she brought one
arm up and covered her head as the Indian fell forward, half across her body. The lance quivered in the
air as he twitched, groaned a last grating gasp, and lay
still.

Fargo reached them and used the end of the lance
to pull the lifeless form aside. Then he yanked the
brave's lance out of the ground. Hope leapt to her
knees, threw both arms around his waist, and clung to
him. "Oh, God, oh, God," he heard her murmur and
finally pulled her to her feet.

"Be grateful on your own time," he snapped. "Let's
go." There was nothing to be gained by hiding tracks
any longer and he set off in a fast trot, holding himself
back to let Hope keep up. He glanced once more at
the forest of silent lifelessness when he reached the
other side. It seemed to reach out after him, unseen,
unheard tentacles of dark anger floating through the
air, unspoken accusations from another world. "Run,"
he snapped. "Let's get the hell out of here."

She raced after him as he broke into a long, loping
stride. He kept to the center of the pass, a long,
snow-covered ribbon of paleness. He reached her horse
first, but moved on as she stopped to untie the animal
and climb into the saddle. He had reached the Ovaro
before she rode up to him and he motioned to her as
he set off at a gallop. He kept the horse going full out
through the darkness, taking the curves of Blood Pass
as if it were a racecourse. He slowed to a canter when
the first gray dawn broke into the night sky. The pace
was reduced to a trot as the dawn spread itself over

the land. No sun, he noted bleakly, the sky still gray with snow hanging behind the clouds.

"I have to rest," he heard Hope call, so he pulled the Ovaro under a tall Canada balsam alongside the pass. The wagons would be making much slower time, but they'd had more than a day's head start, he pondered. "Two hours' rest," he said, and slid from the pinto. He set out his bedroll and Hope gathered herself inside it with him at once. She was asleep the moment her eyes closed.

When he woke he knew they'd slept closer to three hours, the freshness inside his body furnishing the proof. The sky was still leaden and he saw no break anywhere in it as he started down the pass, this time at a slow trot. The thin layer of snow had been enough to cover the wagon tracks for a while, but he finally saw the wheel marks appear and he hurried the pace.

The day was sliding behind the high mountain peaks when he caught sight of the wagons encamped in a little glen. The others came running as he rode into the campsite with Hope. He saw Vera's eyes on her, waiting, and Hope slid from her horse and hurried into the Conestoga with the woman.

"I'd about given you up for lost," Gabe Hazzard said.

"Almost," Fargo grunted.

Abel Gunnard, Harriet holding him by one arm, watched with a hint of reproof in his face. "You make it through?" Abel asked.

"Yes and no," Fargo replied, and drew a frown. "They'll be coming after us," he said. "We'd best make plans. I give them another day to catch up." He turned a glance at Ma Cowley and Cassie, still tied, leaning against their wagon. "They give you any trouble?" he asked.

"No, but Vera kept wanting to wait or go back herself," the foreman answered.

"Hope's brought the answer to her," Fargo said. He added nothing else, and that said more than words.

"We shot a mountain goat. Stewed it real good with

a lot of pepper and onions. Real tasty," Abe Jones said as he stirred a pot over a small cookfire. He poured a plate full for Fargo, and the big man nodded gratefully. The meal tasted as though it were a dollar steak in Kansas City, and Fargo ate hungrily. When he was finished, Hope emerged from the Conestoga and came to him.

"The wondering's done with for her," she said. "I hope it'll change things now. She thanks you for all you did."

"I just hope it's not too late," he said.

When Hope finished her meal, Fargo rose and scanned the others seated around the dying fire. Gabe Hazzard and four left of his crew made five. Gunnar and Harriet made it seven. Ma Cowley and Cassie would have to be freed to fight. That made nine. Ten with himself. He'd send Vera on with the boys and Hope to help her. His lips pursed in thought. There'd be at least twenty Nez Percé warriors, maybe thirty. They'd not clear everyone from camp with winter imminent. But he grimaced at the prospect, a handful of ragtail opponents against at least twenty fierce warriors. He had to find some way to bring down the odds, Fargo knew, anything to give them a chance at survival.

He took his bedroll down, stretched out, and let thoughts tumble through his mind until exhaustion forced sleep on him. When daylight broke still gray and cold, he rose and woke the others. "Let's roll. Every damn minute counts," he barked.

He was waiting in the saddle as they gathered themselves. North along the pass the mountains were silent, the Nez Percé not in sight yet. But they were coming, he told himself bitterly. They had to come. They had to keep faith with the spirits of their dead. All he had to do was keep faith in staying alive. With a harsh snort, he turned the Ovaro and sent the horse down the road.

He heard the others start to follow and he kept a steady pace, his eyes sweeping the terrain on both sides of the pass. He allowed only a half-hour's rest at midday. It was a luxury the Nez Percé wouldn't allow themselves, he knew, but a goose can't be an eagle, he realized.

The day had begun to slide toward an end when he reined up, his mouth a grim slit across his handsome countenance as he surveyed the land to the right of the pass. It was the place he'd marked in his mind and he'd find no better, he knew. The mountain crags rose up behind a series of gulleys and draws, most of stone with a mountain-scrub covering, and he rode from the road to explore the terrain.

When the wagons rolled to a halt he had made his decision. It was one they'd live or die with, he realized, and waved the wagons into a cleared circle a few yards from the pass.

"Everything as usual," he said to Abe Jones as the man made a small fire and began to prepare a meal. Fargo moved onto a flat rock and let his eyes slowly move across the high land. Twilight began to lower itself when he stepped down to where the others had started to gather around the fire. "Company," he announced with matter-of-fact casualness, and saw the others spin to stare up into the high land where the line of near-naked warriors had come into view. He counted ten spread across one ridge and watched as another ten rode into view atop an adjoining ridge. Fargo saw the darkness moving quickly down the mountainside and stepped toward the fire. "I'm hungry," he said. "Let's eat."

Abel Gunnard turned to him, confusion and fear in his face. "Now?" he asked.

"They'll wait till morning," Fargo said. "There's only a few minutes' light left."

"We going to run for it after it gets dark?" Abel Gunnard asked.

"No. They'll only come after us in the morning and catch us someplace where we'll be sitting ducks. This is the best spot for us to make a stand," Fargo said.

"You've got some idea in your head," Gabe Hazzard said, and Fargo nodded.

"Tell you come morning," Fargo said.

"What about us?" Ma Cowley cut in. "You just going to leave us tied up to be killed?"

"No, we'll need every gun we can get. We'll untie you, but not till morning, just in case you get some boneheaded idea to run during the night," Fargo said. "Now let's eat."

The others sat down with nervous glances at the hills above, but the blackness had settled in and only the darker bulk of the peaks remained visible. The meal was taken quickly and in silence. When it was over Fargo went to where Vera had begun to shepherd the boys into the Conestoga. Ted and Tim greeted him with instant hugs and his arms stayed around the two small bodies as he spoke to Vera. "You're going on with the boys tonight," he said. "Hope goes with you," he added as he saw Hope approaching.

"I'll stay here," Hope said.

"You'll go with the boys and Vera. I'd like to see someone come out of this alive. The boys deserve that much."

"What about you?" Hope asked, searching his face with her round brown eyes.

"If I make it, I'll catch up to you," he answered. "You follow the pass back down, the way we came up."

"What about the Blackfoot?" Hope asked.

"They'll be digging in for the winter. It's not likely they'll be riding the hills. But just to be safe, rest during the day and travel by moonlight," he said, and cast a glance at the night sky where the moon remained all but hidden. "If Mother Nature lets you, you'll make it out of the pass by week's end," he said.

Vera nodded gravely and took the boys into the wagon. Hope waited, stepped to him, and slid her arms around his neck. Her lips found his, sweetness in the kiss and the embrace. "For Vera," she murmured.

"Tell her thanks." He smiled. "Now get ready to roll."

When Vera stepped onto the driver's seat a short while later, he watched from the side of the encampment. Abel Gunnard and Harriet emerged at the sound as the Conestoga began to roll, and Gabe Hazzard sat up in his blanket. They all looked on in silence that was fashioned as much of sadness as of grimness. They turned away when the Conestoga disappeared into the night.

Fargo set out his bedroll, stretched out, and set his inner alarm clock to the waking hour he wanted before letting sleep engulf him. A small flurry of snowflakes woke him once during the night, but he returned to sleep when he saw it was nothing more than that.

It was the hanging hours just before dawn when he woke, refreshed himself with his canteen, and put his bedroll away. He started to walk to where Gabe Hazzard slept, his crew nearby, when the figure came from behind the tree trunk. He halted and heard the oath drop from his lips.

"I came back," she said simply. "Vera and the boys are making good time by now."

"Don't you ever do what you're told?" he growled.

"You'll need every gun you can get. I know how to shoot," she said.

"Conscience digging at you?" he said harshly.

"That's most of it. You'd all have been on your way days ago if I hadn't tried to cross the burial grounds. I can't change what's been done, but I can help face the consequences," she said.

"What's the rest of it?" he asked.

"You," she said. "I owe you most of all. If it all goes wrong, I'd like to be lying next to you. If it goes right, I damn well want to be lying next to you."

"Fair enough." He grinned and brushed past her to wake Gabe Hazzard. The man sat up as Fargo went to Gunnard's wagon and rapped against the sides. "Up and out," he muttered. He waited for Gabe's men to finish putting on their gear, and when they were ready,

Abel and Harriet emerged. "Get a rifle for her," he told Gunnard. "And another for Ma Cowley." The man disappeared into the wagon and came out with the two rifles. "You take my Sharps," Fargo said to Hope. She hurried to the pinto while his glance went to the sky where the first streaks of gray had started to slide through the night. "Untie Ma Cowley and Cassie," he ordered, and Abe Jones climbed into the high-sided wagon and emerged with the huge woman and Cassie.

"It's about time," Ma Cowley snapped, and caught the rifle Fargo tossed at her.

"What about me?" Cassie asked. "Don't I get a gun?"

"Not now. I've other plans for you, honey," he said. He pointed to a gulley some fifty yards distant and the others followed his gaze. A narrow mouth, barely wide enough for two horses to enter at once, widened into a long, narrow gulley with mountain brush on each side. "We've got to break them into two groups so they won't overrun us all at once. I want one group trapped in that gulley." He began to outline his plan in terse sentences. When he was finished, it was Gabe Hazzard who asked the question.

"It might just work," he said. "Except for one thing. How do you figure to get half of them into that gulley?"

Fargo smiled and turned to Cassie. "Little Cassie's going to do what she does best, ride around naked."

"What?" Cassie blurted out.

"You heard me," Fargo snapped, and flicked a glance at the sky. "And I don't have time to argue. They're men, just like the rest of us. They'll be curious and eager, just like all the others were. Including me," he added wryly. "They'll follow you—a good number of them at least. You lead them into the gulley. If they start to race at you, you race on too, but you take them into that gulley, you understand?"

"I'll freeze riding naked in this weather," Cassie said.

"It won't take that long," Fargo said.

"It's too cold. I'll turn blue," she insisted.

"The cold will make your tits bigger. Look on the positive side of things," Fargo said. "Get your horse."

Cassie hesitated and looked at Ma Cowley, and the huge woman stayed silent. "Damn you, Ma Cowley," Cassie spit out.

"It's his show." The woman shrugged.

"You going to get your clothes off and get on that horse?" Fargo asked. "Or do I have to tear them off for you and tie you onto the saddle?"

"Bastard," Cassie flung at him as she went to her horse, flung the wool jacket off, slid out of the one-piece dress, and climbed naked onto the horse.

An instant wood sprite, Fargo muttered to himself, all slender, tiny-breasted elfin loveliness. "Ride," he growled. "Up toward that first ridge. They'll be waking soon, daylight's coming in full. I want you up where they'll see you."

Cassie turned the horse and began to ride up the slope toward a ridgeline that lay just beneath the upper one.

Fargo turned to the others. "You know what to do. Let's move," he snapped. Hope came alongside him as he hurried to the line of heavy scrub brush at the base of a thick cluster of spruce. The trees faced the mouth of the gulley and he saw Gabe Hazzard and his men run toward the high-sided farm wagon. Gunnard and Harriet followed him and Ma Cowley puffed her way up last. He'd left Gunnard's rack-bed wagon out by itself where it would draw attention. As he settled down in the thick brush, the others took their positions, Hope kneeling on one knee next to him. "You're supposed to be a dozen feet away from me," he growled.

"In a minute," she said.

Fargo's eyes moved up the slope to where Cassie had reached the lower ridge and halted. As he watched, the first line of Nez Percé appeared on the ridge above her. The Indians stared down at her. He swung his glance to the left, but the second line he had seen last night did not appear. He grunted. "Get to your position," he told Hope, and she moved sideways, settling down behind the scrub brush. Fargo moved his eyes to the other side of the encampment. The second group of Nez Percé would be racing in at it from the other side of the pass, their aim to trap their victims in a cross fire.

Fargo brought his eyes back to the high ridge as Cassie began to move her horse along the ridge below in the direction of the gulley. He waited a moment more and smiled in satisfaction as the line of Nez Percé started to move down toward Cassie. She put her horse into a slow trot and he watched the Indians reach the low ridge and fall in a dozen yards behind her. She saw them with a backward glance and put her horse into a fast trot. She was doing well, Fargo saw, but she realized this was the most important decoy she'd ever play.

The line of braves sent their ponies into a trot and Fargo counted six of them. Less than half, but more than enough to lessen the odds. Cassie was getting closer to the entrance to the gulley when the Nez Percé suddenly put their ponies into a gallop. Cassie heard the sound of it and sent her horse full out without turning to look back. They were close behind her when she raced through the narrow entranceway to the gulley, looking like a frightened wood nymph. The line of Nez Percé raced in after her.

Fargo's lips soundlessly barked the command. The high-sided farm wagon began to roll, Abe Jones at the reins. The man used the whip and the team of horses drove upward to the narrow mouth of the gulley. With a shout, Abe Jones pulled the wagon to a halt across the narrow entranceway and Fargo heard the shouts of anger and surprise from inside the gulley. The trapped Nez Percé had turned from Cassie to race at the wagon. From inside the high-framed body, Gabe and his men exploded a fusillade of shots. They were cutting the Indians in ribbons as the men tried to charge the narrow entranceway, the funneled firepower a merciless barrage.

But another sound interrupted, the wild whoops and thudding hoofbeats of the rest of the Nez Percé racing across the pass and into the camp. A half-dozen circled Gunnard's wagon, pouring arrows into it while the others raced at the wagon that blocked the entrance to the gulley. As they neared it, they crossed in front of the line of thick scrub brush and spruce.

"Fire," Fargo yelled, and the hail of bullets exploded from the brush. He saw the one he'd singled out topple from his racing horse, and he shifted the gunsights and brought down another. Out of the corner of his eye he saw two more horsemen go down. Now the others who had halted to attack the wagon realized they'd been duped. They came racing forward, only a few moving toward the wagon, the rest coming toward where he and the others fired from the brush.

They charged head-on and Fargo drew a bead on one and blasted the Indian's chest open with an almost point-blank shot. The red men had to slow when they reached the trees, and Fargo brought down another one as the Indian paused to find a target. The sharp rustle of brush to his right made him half-turn.

Gunnard and Harriet tried to flee deeper into the spruce. "No, stay down and keep firing," he yelled, but Gunnard was running, Harriet at his side. Fargo saw a half-dozen Nez Percé spread out and race into the trees after them. He fired and reduced the pursuers by one, whirled around as he heard the big Sharps go off to his right and he saw the brave on foot, one arm still upraised with a tomahawk in hand. But the Indian's stomach was a hole that poured red and he collapsed in a heap to lie still.

"Much obliged," he called to Hope, and saw the high-sided wagon begin to roll away from the mouth of the gulley, make a circle, and come back down toward where the rack-bed stood riddled with arrows. He glimpsed the small pyramid of bodies that clogged the entranceway to the gulley as he rose to his feet and motioned to Hope. She rose to follow him down the slope.

"Wait for me, goddammit," he heard Ma Cowley shout. The woman's huge bulk rose from the brush and hurried down after them. Below, the wagon had halted and Gabe Hazzard and his men poured out.

"There are still five in the spruce chasing Abel and Harriet," Hope reminded him.

"There's more than that, goddammit," Fargo rasped as the band of Nez Percé burst from the trees on the other side of the pass. He counted six and saw the tall, thin, weathered form among them. Always a fox, Walking Tree had held some of his braves back for the right moment. He had found it.

Fargo flung Hope to the ground, dropped half over her, and pulled her under the wagon. He managed to get a bead on two of the racing horsemen and sent both toppling from their horses in quick succession. Hazzard dived behind one of the wagon wheels, but Fargo saw two of his crew go down with a half-dozen arrows through them. He swung his body around as the Nez Percé raced by and started coming back on the other side. Gabe managed to dive around to the other wheel and reload, and he emptied his gun as the Nez Percé made another pass. One of the braves went down, Fargo saw, and he got off a shot that sent still another swerving away with his shoulder shattered.

He looked around for Ma Cowley as the Indians rode on to the end of the encampment, halted, and regrouped. The woman's mountainous form lumbered across the ground to the rack-bed wagon. Somehow, she had avoided being struck by an arrow. Now she pulled herself onto the wagon and with a shout sent the horses into a gallop. She swung the heavy wagon onto the pass and sent it racing downward and Fargo looked up to see the five horsemen come out of the spruce. Two objects waved in the wind, tied together by a length of rawhide and hung from the rope bridle of the first horse. One was brown and sparse, the other a brassy yellow.

"I'm going to be sick," Fargo heard Hope gasp.

"You're going to be quiet," he ordered, and watched as the other band of Nez Percé, led by Walking Deer, raced to join those that had come from the spruce. They raced onto the pass together and turned downward.

"We wait a spell. Then we can leave," Fargo said, and crawled out from beneath the wagon.

"How do you know they won't be back to finish us?" Gabe Hazzard said.

"She pulled the lance out of the ground," Fargo said. "They'll be satisfied." He looked around and cursed softly.

Abe Jones pulled himself to his feet. He was the only one that moved.

"Goddamit, I'm freezing," the voice interrupted, and Fargo turned to see Cassie hurrying down the slope from the gulley, her thin arms wrapped around herself. "I had to crawl over all those damn Indians blocking the entranceway."

She had turned a light blue, Fargo noted, and her tits did seem larger. Gabe Hazzard yanked a blanket out of the wagon and draped it around her.

"We'll find something for you to put on later," he said.

"I'll find something," Cassie snapped, and crawled into the wagon.

Fargo walked to where he'd left the Ovaro and brought Hope's horse back with him.

"I'll drive," Abe Jones said, and took the reins as Gabe Hazzard crawled up alongside him. Fargo brought the Ovaro around to the front and walked the horse slowly onto the pass, keeping it at a walk as he turned downward.

"That's all?" Hope asked as she swung in beside him.

"I'd say there's been more than enough," Fargo answered.

"Of course, but it's all over so suddenly," she said. "Shouldn't we stay, do the proper things?"

"Sometimes the only proper thing left is to stay alive. Nothing else, just leave and stay alive," Fargo said. He cast an eye skyward where the gray clouds still waited. But they'd continue to wait, he felt certain. Mother Nature was being kind, her own way of rewarding not the brave but those strong enough to survive.

Fargo stayed silent as they rode until the band of horsemen appeared in front of them. Hope still held the big Sharps and he motioned to her. She handed the rifle to him and he let it rest, the stock held under his armpit, his finger on the trigger as he halted the Ovaro. Walking Deer sat the first horse and the Indian chief's face was hard as stone. But Fargo knew he saw the rifle was pointed directly at him.

"There's been enough killed," Fargo said. "The great spirits will be satisfied. It's over."

"So is the friendship that once we had, Fargo," the Nez Percé chief said. "You did not keep my trust."

"I know," Fargo said. "I am sorry for it. But I had other things to keep. A man must keep what is in his heart."

The Indian eyed the rifle again. "I know what is in your heart now," he said.

Fargo nodded again. "I am sorry for that, too," he said. "But it is there."

Walking Deer let a moment go by before he raised one hand and motioned to his braves.

Fargo kept the rifle on him until he moved past the wagon with slow deliberation. "Roll," he murmured to Abe Jones, and the wagon moved forward. Fargo heard the deep sigh of relief escape Hope's lips and he smiled grimly. "The end of a beautiful friendship," he said.

He found the rack-bed wagon a mile or so on. Ma Cowley still sat in the driver's seat but her bulk was lumped to one side. Fargo remembered how, a long time ago, he had seen a huge sow that had tangled with two porcupines. She lay with hundreds of quills sticking out all over her body. The only difference was that these quills had feathers at the ends.

He moved on and set the pinto into a trot. The night brought exhausted sleep and the days that followed brought hard riding, with only a few stops to rest. They caught up to Vera and the Conestoga as they reached the foot of the mountains and halted to exchange happiness.

"We'll go on with her," Gabe Hazzard said. Fargo nodded as Hope came to his side. They'd look after Cassie, too, he was certain.

Fargo gazed back up at the narrow ribbon that rose up into the Bitterroot Mountains. "Blood Pass," he murmured. "The name couldn't be more appropriate."

"Make me forget, Fargo," Hope said.

"That'll take a lot of nights," he said, smiling, and she smiled back.

"That's the best thing I've heard in a long time." She sighed.

He urged the pinto forward, eager to begin forgetting.

LOOKING FORWARD

**The following is the opening
section from the next novel in the exciting
Trailsman series from Signet:**

THE TRAILSMAN #81
TWISTED TRAILS

*1861, the Montana land,
not even a territory yet, where
the law was what men made it and
life was often measured by the
length of an Indian arrow . . .*

Something was wrong, the big man knew as he reined
his horse to a halt. His lake-blue eyes narrowed as he
peered through the night at the ranch house. A big
house, he noted, long and wide with a second floor
over one half. And the building blazed with light from
every window, the way a house looked when there was
a big party going on inside. But there wasn't a sound
in the night, no voices, no laughter, not the clink of
glasses, no strains of music. Only a tomblike silence.

The big man muttered to himself and moved his
magnificent black-and-white Ovaro forward with slow,
cautious steps. He drew closer to the ranch house and
saw that the front door hung open and the sign at the
outer gate—SAM WHITFORD—CIRCLE Z—had told him
he had the right place. He halted again and slid from
the saddle, now just in front of the porch.

The silence remained absolute. One hand resting on

the butt of the big Colt in its holster, Skye Fargo stepped into the doorway of the house and raised his voice. "Anybody home?" he called out, and felt slightly foolish in view of the bright lights all around him.

But only silence answered. He stepped into the house and found himself in a spacious foyer with a black-and-white tile floor. Beyond the foyer, the house opened into a large living room and he slowly took in large leather couches, a fine cherrywood table and solid chairs, sporting prints hanging from the walls along with fine drapes. It was the living room of a wealthy man, and amid the fine furnishings he saw a silver tray on a side table with three partly filled glasses atop it. The tray seemed waiting to be cleared away.

Fargo moved farther into the house. "Anybody here?" he called again, and again only silence answered. He stepped through a side doorway of the large room and found himself in a study where bookshelves lined the wall along with stuffed antelope heads. A heavy desk occupied the center of the room, a lamp burning brightly atop it, and Fargo started to turn away when he halted and brought his eyes back to the desk.

A man's foot protruded from under one corner. Fargo's long, powerful legs took him to the desk in three strides. He went around to the rear of the desk and stared down at the man who lay facedown on the floor, almost under a chair that had been pushed aside. Blood seeped through the back of the velvet jacket where two knife wounds had torn jagged holes in the garment. The man's thick, silver-white hair was spattered with red and Fargo reached down and half-turned the figure on its side. His lips drew back tightly as he stared down at a face that had been brutally bludgeoned and now lay almost covered with blood. No swift blow to the head but a vicious beating, Fargo noted. The dead man was unquestionably Sam Whitford, his thick mane of silver-white hair unmistakable.

Fargo rose and his lake-blue eyes narrowed as they swept the room. Nothing else was disturbed, at least nothing he could discern. He moved from the dead man, out of the study, and crossed a well-lighted, wide corridor to halt at a kitchen. Stacks of dishes were piled up on the sideboards, along with the remains of brown betty and blueberry pie. There had to have been a party, he murmured inwardly, and there was one more way to prove it. He started to turn when he heard the sound first, a gasped groan. It came again and he strode to where it emanated from behind the kitchen table. Another figure lay on the floor, a woman's figure, a gray-haired, ample form that was clothed in a housemaid's uniform of a black dress with a white apron across the front.

He knelt down and saw the red that leaked through her dress. Her eyes flickered open and she seemed to focus on him. Her lips moved but only a small bubble of red came from them.

"Easy, now, ma'am," Fargo said. "Who did this?"

The woman's eyes seemed to focus on him and she tried to form words, but her torn lungs hadn't breath enough left. All she could manage was a last, gasped groan before her eyes flickered shut again, this time to remain closed.

"Damn," Fargo muttered, and pushed himself to his feet. He walked from the room, crossed the corridor, and strode from the house to the Ovaro. He dropped to one knee and scanned the ground in the light that came from the windows. The wagon tracks were plain, at least six sets of wheel prints, perhaps eight, he noted, and rose to his feet. They completed the picture, at least part of it. There had indeed been a party, with guests who came and left by wagon. That likely meant womenfolk, couples invited for a social gathering. But when the party ended, someone had killed the host. Whoever did it had killed the housemaid, too, probably because she'd seen him. The killer had planned one murder and had to commit the second out of hasty necessity.

Fargo turned and started to go back into the house when the pounding of hoofbeats erupted in the night and the band of riders emerged out of the blackness, horses at a full gallop. He counted seven riders, a tall man with a hatchet jaw in the lead.

The leader fastened his eyes on Fargo as he skidded his horse to a halt. "There he is. Get him," he yelled and drew his six-gun.

Fargo flung himself sideways, crashed into the edge of the door, and rolled into the house as the fusillade of bullets smashed bits of wood from the doorjamb. He sprang to his feet just inside the house, his own Colt in hand, and saw another volley of shots slam into the doorway. He ran into a side corridor and down the narrow passageway.

"After him," he heard the hatchet-jawed man bark and he saw the figures begin racing through the doorway into the house.

Fargo swerved down a side hallway and raced to reach the next corner just as a man appeared from around the other end. The man started to bring his gun up but Fargo smashed the barrel of the Colt into his face and he went down with an oath of pain. Fargo started down another adjoining corridor and saw two more figures appear at the far end. They knew the house, whoever they were, he saw, and he dropped to one knee as the two men raised their six-guns. He fired twice and both men flew backward to smash into the wall. They seemed to be holding hands as they slid to the floor.

At the sound of footsteps behind him, Fargo whirled and dived to one side all at the same time. The shot passed over his head by less than an inch and he felt the rush of air from the bullet. His own shot hit the man full in the midsection and he pitched forward, both hands clasped to his abdomen. Fargo was running before the man hit the ground. He leapt over the groaning form, spied the staircase, and raced for it.

The Trailsman took the steps three at a time, reached the second-floor landing, paused to look down, and saw the hatchet-jawed man and two others at the bottom of the steps. He threw a quick shot downward and the men ducked back. Fargo spun away from the top of the stairs to see that the second-floor corridor formed a dead end with two rooms at the far side, but he also spotted the gabled window in the middle of the hall. He ran for it while footsteps pounded up the stairway behind him. The small window led directly onto the roof and he yanked it open, pushed one long leg through its narrow opening, pulled the rest of himself after it, and paused for a moment. The rooftop had a slight slant to it and he started to scurry across the shingles to the edge, where he halted again. He saw the front of the house almost directly below him, the Ovaro to one side of the doorway, the other horses opposite.

"There he is," he heard someone shout and glanced across the rooftop to the window where two heads peered out.

"Shoot, dammit," the hatchet-jawed man barked, and Fargo threw himself flat on the rooftop as a shot whistled by. He let himself roll, grabbed the edge of the roof, and let his long frame hang down. He dangled for a moment and heard the others hurrying across the roof. He let his hands open and dropped, his body braced, and though he landed on the balls of his feet, he still felt the shock waves go through him. He let his knees bend, paused for another moment to let muscles spring back, and threw a glance upward. The man's head appeared at the edge of the roof but Fargo had the Colt raised and waiting. He pressed the trigger and the man screamed as he toppled face-forward from the roof.

Fargo heard the dull, crunching thud as the man hit

the ground, but he was already racing for the Ovaro. He leapt onto the horse and the Ovaro, ever sensitive to touch and mood, went into a gallop immediately. Three more shots followed him into the night, all wild and far off target.

Fargo followed the road for a hundred yards and then swerved right to climb a low hill thick with red ash and buckeye. He kept riding until he came to a place where the hill leveled off, and he reined to a halt and slid from the saddle. He lowered himself against the light-brown bark of a thick red ash and allowed himself the luxury of a long, deep breath.

This had not been the kind of reception he'd expected or wanted. For two weeks he had been riding to meet with Sam Whitford, only to find the man brutally murdered along with his housemaid. Fargo let the gruesome scene hang in his mind again, mentally reviewing everything he had observed. He had wanted to return inside the house for a closer look when the night riders had arrived. The frown clung to his brow. The men hadn't just happened by. They'd asked no questions, given him no time to explain anything. They had come expecting and aiming to kill.

A cascade of questions raced through his head. He had to start at the beginning, at that first meeting with Sam Whitford that had eventually brought him here. He put his head back against the tree, closed his eyes, and let that time spring into his consciousness in its every detail.

He'd been in Independence Rock down in Wyoming Territory, where he'd just finished a job for John Anderson. It had been John who'd brought Sam Whitford to him and Fargo remembered how he'd been at once impressed by the man's suave manners, the silver-white hair above a face that still retained youth, and a sharp-eyed steely quality. "John told me you were the very best," Sam Whitford had said. "And you're contracted to break trail for Ed Simmons, all the way down to New Mexico Territory."

"I am," Fargo had said.

"That'll take you into next month," the man remarked.

"It will." Fargo nodded as curiosity poked at him.

"Then you'll be ready when I need you," Sam Whitford said, and took out a roll of bills. He peeled off a sizable number and pushed them at the big man across from him. "Five hundred dollars, to seal the deal and ensure you're taking the job for me," he said.

"That's a powerful lot of walking money," Fargo commented.

"It is, but there'll be a powerful lot of work to do," the man said, and ran a palm through the thick silver-white hair.

"What kind of work?" Fargo asked.

Sam Whitford smiled. "I never spell out my plans till I'm ready to move on them," he said.

"That's smart," Fargo said.

"But it looks as though I'm going to have to do some manhunting and I'll need the very best trailsman in the West," Sam Whitford said.

"Fair enough," Fargo said, and pushed the bills into his pocket.

"My ranch, the last day of next month," Sam Whitford said. "In Montana, west of Crazy Peak. There's a town called Horsehead. Take the road north some three miles to a broken, crooked, bare-branched elm and turn left. You'll come to my place, the Circle Z."

"I'll be there," Fargo said, and that had been the heart of it. They'd talked some about mutual acquaintances and then Sam Whitford had gone his way, leaving the kind of money you didn't turn down without some damn good reason.

And now, Fargo frowned, the man who had hired him, paid him that good money, had been brutally killed and he'd been damn near shot. He wasn't about to turn away and hightail it, not after a posse of gunslingers had tried to cut him down without so much as a question. He felt a certain obligation to Sam Whitford, certainly to his kin, and he supposed there were some. A wealthy man such as Sam Whitford plainly was, usually had kin. He'd stay, Fargo decided, until he got a few answers of his own. He owed that much to the man who hired him, dead or alive.

He rose, took down his bedroll, undressed, and stretched out in it. There were things he'd noted about the murder itself, and maybe they were tied in to what Sam Whitford had said when hiring him. Maybe. But there was too little yet to do anything but waste time on fruitless wonderings, and Fargo decided that sleep was much the better course and he closed his eyes. Morning would be time enough to arrange his first steps.

He slept well, the night quiet, the red ash a thick leafy ceiling over his head. He woke when the morning sun filtered its way down through the foliage. He sat up and the events of the night were on him at once. He made plans as he washed and dressed, found a stand of sweet elder, and breakfasted on the berries. He'd seek out kin first, Fargo decided, and perhaps the best place for that would be the sheriff in Horsehead. He'd also tell the man what he'd found and how he'd been set on.

Fargo turned the Ovaro down the slope, reached the road below, and made a wide circle around the Whitford ranch. He paused to look down on it from a distant hill and saw only a few horses tethered near a corral and he rode on after a moment. He had skirted the town during the night when he rode to reach the Circle Z Ranch, but he'd noted it was not unlike a thousand other towns, perhaps a little bigger than most. That assessment was reinforced as he rode into its wide main street and slowed the Ovaro to a walk. Horsehead had the usual collection of farm wagons, some big Owensboro mountain wagons with their oversize brakes, and one bare-poled timber wagon.

He rode past a general store, a barbershop, a black-smith, and just past the center of town, a small bank. A dance hall with the name CARRIE'S BUNKHOUSE over the front door came into view, all places common enough in a town, but he was surprised to see a church with a thin steeple and a long grain supply shed nearby. He wondered if the presence of the Sioux and Crow throughout the land accounted for even the church being centered in town. He was beginning to wonder about the sheriff's office when he came to it almost at the other end of town, a thin, frame building with a single window and a long hitching post outside.

He rode to a halt, swung from the Ovaro to see the man emerge, a sheriff's badge on his checkered shirt and behind him a thinner figure sporting a deputy's badge. The sheriff was a medium-sized man with an oversized, bulbous nose, heavy-knuckled hands, and shrewd eyes that stared at him, flicked to the Ovaro and back to him, Fargo saw. The Trailsman glimpsed the thinner man move to one side, circle toward a horse tied to the hitching post. The sheriff continued to stare at him, Fargo saw, a frown digging into the man's face. "You come to see me, mister?" the man asked.

"I did," Fargo said. "If you're the sheriff here."

"I am. Sheriff Al Johnson," the man said. "You wouldn't have been at Sam Whitford's place last night, would you, mister?"

"Just so happens I was," Fargo said. He heard the click of a hammer being drawn back, glanced to where the deputy held a six-gun trained on him. He glanced back and saw the sheriff had pulled a Smith & Wesson Model I and leveled it at him. Fargo stared at the seven-shot, single-action weapon for a moment and returned his eyes to the bulbous-nosed face. "What the hell's this all about?" he growled.

"You're under arrest, mister," the sheriff said, "for the murder of Sam Whitford."

RAY HOGAN KEEPS THE WEST WILD